RANDOM ACCESS MURDER

Random Access Murder
Copyright © 2023 by Carol Gandolfo

Published in the United States of America
ISBN   Paperback: 979-8-89091-354-8
ISBN   eBook: 979-8-89091-355-5

All rights reserved. No part of this publication may be reproduced, stored in a retrieval system or transmitted in any way by any means, electronic, mechanical, photocopy, recording or otherwise without the prior permission of the author except as provided by USA copyright law.

The opinions expressed by the author are not necessarily those of ReadersMagnet, LLC.

ReadersMagnet, LLC
10620 Treena Street, Suite 230
San Diego, California, 92131 USA
1.619. 354. 2643 | www.readersmagnet.com

Book design copyright © 2023 by ReadersMagnet, LLC. All rights reserved.

Cover design by Ericka Obando
Interior design by Don De Guzman

RANDOM ACCESS MURDER

CAROL GANDOLFO

CHAPTER ONE

The presentation set for today would determine if the team would be labeled as heroes or villains. It all depended on Nestor.

In a room just off from the lab, Dr. Bethany Middleton sat hunched in front of her computer pecking at the keyboard.

"Beth, are you ready for the presentation?"

Startled, Beth swiveled in her chair to face Dr. William Thornton. He wore a brand new, gray pinstripe suit and freshly ironed white shirt.

"You look nice," she smiled at the man who had been her teacher and mentor for the past ten years.

"Thanks." He paused. "I understand they are setting up now. Are you ready?"

Beth stood and straightened Dr. Thornton's tie. "Yes, I guess we're prepared. Do you think I can have another half an hour? We still need to get Nestor dressed and drive to the courthouse."

"I'm sure I can get you more time," Dr. Thornton replied. "I'll head on over and stall until you get there." Dr. Thornton waved and pushed the button to open the door. James Molans stood just outside.

"Morning," Dr. Thornton said to James then turned back to Beth. "You know, if this works out I'll be able to retire and Barbara and I can finally travel the world."

"Barbara would love that. By the way, tell her thank you for the birthday card." Dr. Thornton moved past James and left.

"Morning, Dr. Thornton. See you at the courthouse," James said and closed the door behind the doctor.

Bethany returned to her computer, tapped on a few more keys then shut it off. She picked up the phone and punched in Cindy's number.

"Cindy, it's time to get Nestor ready. Can you join us in the lab?" When Cindy responded, Beth hung up, crossed the room and stood before a pressurized door. She swiped the security lock and waited while the door slid open with a swishing sound.

Nestor lay on a metal table, a thin sheet covering his naked body. Beth approached him and removed the sheet. She folded it and set it aside. James moved closer and considered Nestor. Together, they inspected him.

A few minutes later, the lab door opened again and Cinderella Takahashi, a small Asian female with shiny black hair in the popular Japanese, Anime-style strolled in. She wore a lab coat too large for her small frame. Her hair and thick glasses covered most of her face. Cinderella, or "Cindy," (she hated the name her fairy tale-obsessed mother had given her) pulled over a step stool and climbed up to get a better view. At only five feet tall, she needed help to study the figure on the table. With a magnifying glass she examined Nestor. When she reached the bulge at the crotch area, she stepped off the stool, retrieved a towel and covered the area between his legs. "Why did we even have to put a lump there?" Without waiting for a response, she continued. "The synthetic skin really looks cool. However, James should have put some imperfections on his face. Like some freckles. His skin is much too perfect."

Beth and James shared a smile as the petite twenty-year old stepped back on her stool.

"I had to make it look like he had genitalia, so he looks like a man." James explained.

"Yeah, I know. Gotta look cool." Cindy's language belied the fact that she received her medical degree in Neurophysiology at the age of sixteen, completed her internship at seventeen and earned a PhD in Computer Engineering only a year later. "Nestor looks ready to kick some butt. Can I test him?"

"Now?" Jim asked.

"Nestor, sit up." Cindy commanded, not waiting for a response.

Nestor swung his legs off the table and came to a sitting position.

"Nestor, stand." He slid off the table and stood in front of Beth. Cindy glanced at James and Beth. "Okay, you try."

Beth considered Nestor. "Nestor, step forward." He took one step forward. "James, your turn."

"Nestor, turn toward me." Nestor faced James.

"He's been programmed for both verbal and telepathic commands. But just the three of us can do it." Cindy pulled a scalpel from her pocket and gazed at her colleagues. "Do you mind?"

Beth hesitated. "We have a meeting in about ten minutes. Can't we wait?"

"I'll do it where no one can see," Cindy said and made a small nick on Nestor's side.

Beth and James moved forward and watched. Slowly, the skin reconnected and in just ten seconds, the quarter-inch cut had completely disappeared.

"Cool. One more," Cindy whined.

"Cindy!"

Too late. Cindy ran the scalpel across Nestor's chest. Beth's eyes rolled as a five-inch slice appeared. They watched as the synthetic skin quickly healed.

"Good job on the skin, James. You're a master."

"Should I get him dressed?" James ignored her remark and moved back from the table.

"Yes, please. His clothes are on the rack. Can you hurry? We need to get out of here in ten minutes to make it on time. Nestor, sit on the table." Beth looked at Nestor. He sat. "Wonderful. Now let's get moving."

"Sure thing, doc. Are you going to change?" James asked.

Beth studied James and realized he was also dressed for the event. He wore a pair of neatly creased beige slacks, a tweed sports jacket, a white shirt and red bowtie. He had shaved off his usual stubble and combed his unruly blond hair.

"Oh, right. Cindy, are you sure you don't want to come?"

Cindy's bowl-shaped haircut swung back and forth. "Heck, no. I just want to stay behind the scenes. Can't stand bureaucrats."

Beth turned back to James. "Nice outfit."

He dropped his head slightly and closed his eyes for several seconds.

"I'm sorry," she reached out and touched his arm.

"No, don't be. You better than anyone understands. I figured it was time I learned to iron my own clothes." He opened his jacket and pointed to a rust-colored triangle on the side of his shirt. "See, only one scorch mark -- but enough about me. You better get ready."

Beth nodded and hurried into her office. She removed her lab coat, hung it on a hook on the back of her door, then pulled a black blazer from the closet and put it on. In her small bathroom, she ran a comb through her long red hair and clipped it in back with a barrette. She applied a small amount of gloss to her full lips and checked herself in the mirror. She could use a bit of mascara but shrugged it off. She grabbed her car keys and briefcase and returned to the lab.

James finished knotting Nestor's bow tie and stood back.

"How does he look?"

Beth walked around Nestor. At five-foot seven inches, he was only slightly taller than she. His light brown hair was combed over to the left. He wore gray slacks and a tweed blazer. His pale gray eyes and too-white skin made him perfect. He appeared average in every way. She took a pair of horn-rimmed glasses from the desk and placed them on his nose.

"I see you dressed him like yourself," She said to James. "He looks pretty harmless. That should make people more comfortable when interacting with him."

James straightened Nestor's bow tie. "You're right. Most people won't even notice him in a crowd. Good job. Now we'd better hurry."

"Nestor, walk."

Beth reached up to straighten James' bowtie. Her hand shook slightly. "You know, you two could pass for brothers."

James took her hand. "Gee, thanks. Just what I need, to look like an android. Hey, are you okay? You look a little nervous."

Beth filled her lungs. "Can't help it. We worked so hard for this day, and I can't believe it's finally here."

Ten minutes later, Beth, James and Nestor opened the door of a small courtroom on the second floor of the U.S. District Court in Washington, D.C.

CHAPTER TWO

Dr. Thornton stopped speaking when the Beth, James and Nestor entered the courtroom.

A semi-circular table sat in the center of the room. Another, smaller table was placed in front with a large screen behind it. A computer sat on the floor next to the smaller table. Two chairs were placed on either side of that table. There were several rows of benches at the back.

Already seated at the large table, from left to right, were the attorney for the prisoner, the United States Attorney General Mark Murphy, a judge appointed by the President and Dr. Thornton. Two empty chairs were reserved for Beth and James. An armed Sheriff stood off to the left side.

Beth walked around the right side of the main table and placed Nestor at the left side of the small table.

Dr. Thornton waited until everyone was seated, then stood. "Gentlemen, I would like to introduce Dr. Bethany Middleton and James Molans, the creators of Nestor." He sat down.

"Thank you, Dr. Thornton." She continued to stand next to Nestor.

"Gentlemen, I would like to introduce you to Nestor. His name stands for Neuropsychological Extra Sensory Tribunal Operational Robot." She turned to Nestor. He stood unmoving. "Nestor is actually an android rather than a robot. His brain operates by using a powerful computer and he can reproduce actual images from inside a human's brain using a functional Magnetic Resonance Imaging scanner. This is essential to the trial phase of the justice program. Nestor can decipher brain activity by measuring blood flow through the brain's visual cortex then reconstruct and display those images. This process becomes critical when considering innocence or guilt of a defendant. Humans are not capable of hiding those images from Nestor. Those thoughts can then be viewed by hooking Nestor up to a monitor. The court will be able to see the actual crime, as it occurred, from the defendant's point of view."

The Attorney General Mark Murphy put up his hand and Dr. Middleton stopped. "How do we focus the defendant in on the particular crime?"

"Any stimuli related to the crime will elicit the thoughts. For example, if you show a photograph of the victim, the defendant is unable to block those thoughts. A visual of the crime will be displayed on the screen in front of you. If the defendant did not commit the crime, then we will be able to see what part he played in it, that is if he was present. If the defendant was not present, Nestor won't display images of the crime and the defendant is presumed innocent."

"Presumed innocent?"

"Of course, there are individuals who participate in a murder for hire. Most won't be able to hide their connection. However, if the individual did not know the person hiring the murder, it will be more difficult for Nestor to read."

"What about the punishment phase of the trial?" the Judge Idleman asked.

"It won't be pleasant to watch, depending on the crime. If guilty, the defendant will have the thoughts relayed back into his brain by Nestor. The result will be a death where the criminal dies imagining himself as the victim. The guilty party will feel the same degree of pain as the victim underwent."

"You stated we would actually watch the crime," the Murphy pointed at the screen.

"Right, that is the most unpleasant part of this. So, you must be prepared." Dr. Thornton sat.

AG Murphy turned to face the attorney for the prisoner, seated next to him. "Mr. Haynes, are you ready to proceed?"

Mr. Haynes stood. "I have one question for Dr. Middleton. How do you communicate with Nestor?"

"We use verbal and telepathic commands. For the verbal commands, Nestor has been programmed to only respond to those on our team. But he can also respond to our thoughts when they are directed toward him. Now I will demonstrate his ability to follow commands." Dr. Middleton stood and motioned to Nestor. "Nestor, stand and walk around to the table then sit down."

Nestor stood, walked to the smaller table and sat down. He waited. Beth went over and connected several electrodes to his scalp and connected them to a computer on the floor. She turned on the computer and the screen above came to life. Satisfied the computer was connected, she relaxed.

She turned to face the panel then peered at the android. "Nestor, raise your right hand."

He raised his right hand and continued stare straight ahead.

"Nestor is now keyed into my mental thoughts. I will give him a command without speaking." *Nestor, put your hand down.*

Nestor put his hand down.

Mr. Haynes picked up a yellow pad. "We are ready to proceed." His chest rose and fell. "Mr. Norris has agreed to allow this procedure to take place and let us view his crimes. Since he has already been convicted, we can use this presentation as evidence of the effectiveness of the program. Mr. Norris has agreed to the punishment phase in lieu of his execution by lethal injection, which was scheduled for last week. We have agreements signed and witnessed by the U.S. Attorney General and the Governor that Mr. Norris' family will receive the amount of one million dollars for his agreement to this form of execution."

"Dr. Middleton," the Murphy said. "You may go ahead with the presentation."

Dr. Middleton walked up to Nestor and checked the electrodes one last time. Using the remote, she turned the computer back on and projected a crime scene photo onto the large screen. Mr. Haynes lowered his head.

"We're ready," she returned to her seat next to Dr. Thornton. He put his large hand over her shaking one. James nudged her with his shoulder and gave her a thumbs up.

"You did well," he whispered. She nodded.

The judge tapped his gavel. "Is everyone ready to begin?" He paused. "Guard, you can bring in the prisoner."

The Sheriff walked across the room and knocked on a door to the right of the group. He tapped four times. Several minutes later, a security guard entered the room with a tall, thin man in an orange prison outfit. He had disheveled dark hair and stubble on his chin. Black, deep-set eyes hidden behind thick, horn-rimmed glasses and bushy eyebrows gave him a frightening appearance. The security guard sat the man across from Nestor. Nestor did not move.

"Remove the handcuffs, please," Dr. Middleton instructed. "Nestor gets a stronger impression when he has physical contact with the subject. The metal may interfere with the transmission."

Both lawyers shifted in their seats but remained quiet when the U.S. Attorney General gave his consent.

"Nestor, trial." Beth commanded.

The U.S. Attorney General raised his hand "Trial?"

"Trial is the prompt word for Nestor to search for either Right or Wrong. Right means there is no criminal connection. Wrong means guilt."

Nestor reached out and took the prisoner's hands in his own. Almost immediately, an image came up on the monitor. There was an audible gasp as the image of a young girl appeared on the screen, her face contorted in pain. Unable to look away, the panel watched in horror as she was tortured, strangled and her throat cut. She bled out, causing the onlookers to turn away. Norris never turned toward the screen. His lips curled slightly as he watched the audience's reaction.

"I think we now have definitive proof of the crime and confirmation of our conviction," the AG Murphy glared at Mr. Norris. "Mr. Norris, you have agreed to the punishment for your crimes and we will honor our commitment to your family. While normally I do not condone any payment to a criminal or his family, you have now given us a way to determine guilt with certainty. This will save the state millions of dollars in future trials. We will now proceed."

Nestor contemplated Norris. The prisoner pulled his hands from the android's grasp and slid to the floor. His body convulsed. The entire panel stood, open mouthed. His body stiffened. He writhed and jerked again. Someone yelled, "Get a doctor."

The guard crossed the space between himself and the flailing Norris and reached down. Norris quickly reached up, grabbed the guard's gun from his holster and pulled the trigger. The guard collapsed onto the floor, red spreading across the front of his khaki uniform. Norris pushed the bailiff away and stood. On the other side of the room, the Sheriff pulled his gun and aimed. He hesitated. Norris turned the gun on the Sheriff and fired. The bullet sliced through the left side of Nestor's skull and hit the Sheriff in the neck. Nestor was thrown back and onto the floor.

The Sheriff grabbed his neck with his left hand and fired with his right, shots spraying wildly. He crumped to the ground. The first bullet struck the Mark Murphy in the back of the neck and severed his spinal cord, killing him instantly. The second bullet hit Judge Idleman in the left side when he stood in an attempt to escape. Judge Idleman fell to the floor.

Norris trained his gun on his attorney and fired. "Some deal, you bastard." The bullet hit Mr. Haynes in the chest, knocking him backwards.

Dr. Thornton grabbed Beth by the upper arm and pulled her to the ground, covering her body with his. Beth hit her head on the edge of the table on the way down and passed out. James jumped up and ran toward the exit. Norris fired again and the next bullet hit James in the shoulder, propelling him forward between two rows of benches. He lay still. Norris walked toward Dr. Thornton, lying atop Beth. He aimed the gun.

Nestor was knocked to the ground when a bullet pierced the side of his head and severed several wires as it traveled through. He then turned onto his front and crawled through the room and toward the exit.

Agent Tom Ford, having finished testifying in another case, passed the door of the courtroom when the first shots sounded. He tried the door. It was locked. He called for backup and kicked at the door. It burst open. He quickly scanned the room and saw several bodies lying on the bloodied carpet. He stepped over one body encased in a tweed jacket. He focused on the prisoner in the orange jumpsuit, who pointed his gun at Dr. Thornton. "Drop it."

Norris laughed and pulled the trigger at the same time as Agent Ford. Beth was unaware a bullet had hit and killed her beloved colleague. Norris' bullet flew past Agent Ford and hit the wall behind him. Ford's bullet hit its mark and Norris flew backwards from the impact to his chest and landed in a sitting position against the back wall.

Agent Ford approached the shooter and kicked away his gun. The killer smiled up at Ford.

"I got to choose my own death," he said. He coughed up a bubble of blood and died.

Behind him, Ford heard a groan and wheeled around. A woman lay mostly hidden beneath the man the convict had shot last. He knelt and pushed off the body and studied the bloodied figure. Her eyes slowly opened, revealing deep green eyes.

"Help is on the way," he said.

She raised her head and tried to get up.

"Better not move till the ambulance arrives."

"I'm not shot," she said and sat up.

"Beth?" A voice sounded behind them.

Ford stood and turned his gun toward the sun. "James?"

Ford put away his gun and found a man in a tweed jacket wedged between two rows of benches.

"Can you help me up?" James asked when he saw Agent Ford. Confused, Ford lifted the bench and helped James to his feet.

"Are you shot?" Ford scanned the slim man, his bow tie askew. He glanced back at the spot near the door where he thought he had stepped over this very person. That was impossible.

"Yes, but I'm pretty sure it went straight through. I think I have a broken collar bone, though."

Ford inspected James, confused.

"I'm a doctor," James explained and got to his feet, holding his left arm.

The door behind them slammed against the wall as a man in uniform aimed his gun at the Ford, Beth and James. Seeing a familiar face, he lowered his weapon.

"What happened here, Tom?"

"Damn if I know."

The Capitol police arrived and the secured the scene. An officer picked up the gun Norris had used and placed it in an evidence bag. EMT's were allowed to enter and tend to the wounded. The judge sustained a head wound and was rushed to the hospital. As the first on the scene, Agent Ford was assigned the investigation.

An EMT checked Beth for injuries and found only a bump on the back of her head. The bullet had passed through the meaty part of James' upper shoulder and the EMT bandaged him and was ready to transport him when Beth sat up on her stretcher and whispered. "Where's Nestor?"

Both scanned the area. James got up off the gurney. "Hey," he said to the EMT. "I have to find my friend." He searched among the seats in the back of the room. Nestor was not among the injured.

Agent Ford walked up, having overhead James. "Is something wrong?"

"We can't find Nestor." Beth continued to scan the room.

"Who?"

"He's not here." James' pushed away the EMT trying to provide first aid. "We have to find him." Panic crept into his voice. Beth grabbed at his good arm and squeezed it.

"Who's Nestor?" Agent Ford persisted.

"Um, you're not cleared." Beth waited, defiantly. She turned and started out the door.

Agent Ford grabbed her arm and turned her back. Her worried eyes regarded his and she went limp. Agent Ford held her up and called over the EMTs. "We need some help here." He turned to James. "You need to tell me about this Nestor."

"I need to make a call first."

CHAPTER THREE

During the confrontation between Agent Ford and the convict, Nestor saw the open door and crawled out of the room. Once outside, he stood and walked to a door with a plaque announcing "STAIRS." He stepped into the stairwell just as the elevator doors opened and several officers spilled out.

Nestor calmly went to the first floor. In the lobby, having heard gunfire, people ignored the nondescript man and ran for cover. He walked past them and left the building as police and ambulance arrived. He found himself outside on the streets of Washington, D.C. A slight breeze ruffled his hair. No trace of the wound was visible, and the synthetic hair had already grown over the small white scar.

Behind him, the courthouse was locked down and police surrounded the building. Nestor continued to walk down the main street, away from the chaos. News reporters arrived in vans and sidewalks crowded with onlookers.

As Nestor walked, he heard a cacophony of voices cascading through the wires of his CPU. A block from the courthouse, he stopped and listened. Through his visual sensors, he watched as a man put his hands around a woman's neck and squeezed. She clawed at his hands as she struggled to breathe. When she could no longer fight, her hands fell limply to her sides. The man squeezed several seconds longer then let her drop to the floor. The man in the dark suit glanced at her dead body and then calmly picked up his car keys from the hallway table and checked himself in the mirror next to the front door. Satisfied he was not mussed; he grabbed his briefcase and left his house.

"*Wrong.*" Nestor homed in on the visual and focused on a man in an expensive three-piece suit. He approached the man and reached out his hand. The man stopped, his brows together, and focused at Nestor. Nestor watched the man and reached out as if to shake his hand.

"Can I help you, young man?"

Nestor said nothing. The man gripped Nestor's offered hand and shook it. "Nice to meet you. What is your name?"

Nestor did not respond.

"Do I know you?" the man asked.

Nestor held the man's hand for a few seconds, reversing the visual and directed it back into the man's mind. He dropped the man's hand and walked away.

"Odd young fellow," the man said to his driver who had just arrived.

"What was that sir?" the driver called through the open window.

"Oh, nothing. Let's head back to my office." The well-known defense attorney reached for the car door and stopped. He clutched at his throat. An intense pressure pushed on his neck muscles. Visions of his choking wife filled his head. He felt his own powerful hands tightening on his windpipe as he gasped. The chauffeur jumped out of the car.

"Mr. Johnson, are you okay?"

Mr. Johnson did not answer. He took one last gasp and died.

"Now it is Right."

Nestor continued to walk along the street. He sensed the thoughts of those around him. *"Right. Right. Right."*

CHAPTER FOUR

Agent Tom Ford and James, his arm now in a sling, sat beside Beth's hospital bed. Beth opened her eyes. "Where am I?"

"You're in the hospital. You slept through the night." Agent Ford offered. "I'm Tom Ford, Special Agent of the FBI."

"Dr. Beth Middleton," she said rising to a sitting position. She studied James and whispered. "Did you find Nestor?"

"Dr. Middleton," Agent Ford interrupted. "I've been briefed."

Beth's turned her eyes to James. She started to speak, then stopped.

"Relax. James and I have already talked to the AG Murphy's office and the President. But you need to calm down." He fluffed her pillow. "Lie back down. It seems you hit your head when Dr. Thornton pushed you down and you are under observation to make sure you don't have a concussion."

Beth lowered her head to the pillow. "Then you know how dangerous this situation is."

"Yes, and I've been assigned to assist you in finding Nestor. Unfortunately, we think he has already run into someone."

"What?" She sat up again. The Agent touched her shoulder. She took a deep breath.

James pulled his chair closer. "They found a criminal attorney dead two blocks away. They thought he had a heart attack, but the coroner said he appeared to have been strangled. Which is odd since witnesses said the last contact, he had with anyone was a nondescript man in his thirties. All the witnesses confirm the only contact was a handshake."

Beth shook her head "Oh, my God. So, you know what that means?"

"Do you mind if I call you Beth?" Tom paused. "Yes, we found out he had murdered his wife that morning and staged it to look like a break-in he could conveniently discover when he got home. Getting back to today, we interviewed all the survivors in the meeting, which is only you, the judge, James and now Nestor."

"Okay?"

"The judge swears he saw Nestor get hit by a bullet and thrown backward. Then it seemed the bullet traveled thru to the Sheriff. After that, the judge got hit and didn't see what happened to Nestor."

James closed his eyes. "If Nestor's wiring is screwed up, no telling what he is going to do."

"Agent, we better get to the lab as soon as possible." Beth said. "We should include Cindy."

"Call me Tom." He moved to help her sit up.

Beth pulled off the blanket and she saw her hospital gown. "Oh."

The two men stood. "We'll call a nurse to help." Tom reached over and pushed the call button. After the nurse had walked in the two men left the room and waited outside.

After one night in the hospital, Beth felt better. Cindy had fawned all over her colleagues until being assured they were fine. Then she cried for Dr. Thornton. Beth consoled her and then introduced her to Tom and explained the situation. When Tom excused himself to use the restroom, Cindy pulled on Beth's arm like an excited child.

"Man, is he hot. Did you notice those amber eyes? They're just like the necklace my mom got me for graduation. My first degree, you know." She blabbered on.

"Calm down, Cindy." Beth patted her arm.

Cindy reverted to her quiet self once Tom returned. The small group convened around a conference table. Beth had to nudge Cindy more than once for staring at Tom.

Tom's phone buzzed constantly. He studied his phone. "I better take this." He got up and walked outside the room. When he returned, he looked at Beth and shook his head. "I think Nestor has struck again. A Senator."

James moaned. Cindy said nothing. Beth stood, ready to leave.

CHAPTER FIVE

Nestor roamed the streets until he found an alley with a dark doorway. He moved back into the recess and closed his eyes. For the next hour, he allowed wiring in his head to start the mending process.

A voice floated through the air. "Nes…"

Nestor opened his eyes and studied his environment.

Nothing.

As the dawn lit the alley he wandered back onto the streets until he stood in front of a large domed structure. People dressed the same as those in the courthouse, walked up and down the steps to the large building. "*Right. Right. Right. Wrong. Wrong.*"

Nestor walked up to someone with *Wrong* emanating from him. The tall gray-haired man held his head high as he towered over a few younger people who hung on his every word. "*Wrong. Wrong.*"

Nestor was drawn to this man. He tilted his head to the side. He took in the visions coming from this man.

A woman gulped for air, though the man didn't touch her. Nestor moved closer. The image was stronger. The woman appeared young. Her long, dark hair floated around her. The man sat beside her as the water covered them both. He struggled out of his seat belt. She reached for him, but he slapped her hand away and pulled himself out the window and up through the water. "*Wrong. Wrong.*" The man did not touch the woman. He did not strangle her. But she died.

"*Wrong*". Nestor approached the man who put out his hand. An aide moved in to intercept Nestor.

"Hey, it's okay. Always here for my fans." The man responded in his thick Bostonian accent and extended his hand. He grasped Nestor's hand. "What's your name, young man?"

Nestor surveyed the older man's rheumy eyes and read his visions. *Wrong.* He dropped the man's hand and examined the four young aides. "*Right. Right. Right.*" He turned and walked away.

"Strange person." The tall man said, then coughed. He coughed again and clutched at his throat. He slumped to the ground in slow motion and gasped. The aides hovered around him as he panted.

"Call an ambulance," one aide yelled. "I think the Senator's having a heart attack." By the time the ambulance arrived, the Senator was dead.

CHAPTER SIX

Agent Ford, Beth and her team sat at a table littered with empty Chinese takeout cartons. The aromas of spices and soy sauce filled the team's lab conference room. Cindy's head rested on her arms. She snored slightly.

"First of all, thanks for meeting me here. We need to figure out how to find Nestor, and, yes, he killed a Senator." He pointed at Cindy. "I think we should go ahead and send her home."

"Don't you dare," Cindy mumbled, her head still on the table. "We need to figure out how to retrieve Nestor. His chip wasn't installed yet, so we have no way to track him. We're going to have to let the police put out a BOLO, you know, a Be On the Look Out."

James shook his head but said nothing.

"Oh, God. That will set off a panic." Beth stood and started to clear the table.

"She's right." Tom gathered several boxes and dirty paper plates, then dropped them into the trash. "We'll need to be careful how we word it. Maybe we can put it out as a person with need of medical care. Maybe amnesia, a head injury, etc."

James slammed his hand on the table. "It's my fault. If only I'd put in the tracking device. I thought I saw Nestor get hit. What if he's damaged?"

Tom touched James on his good shoulder. "You can't spend time blaming yourself. We just need to find him." Tom picked up a can of warm soda and took a sip. "Tell me more about Nestor."

"Well," Beth dropped an empty box into a trashcan, "James and I were working with Dr. Thornton building prosthetics for veterans." She hesitated. "He knew both of us had lost family members to murder and suggested there should be a way to determine guilt or innocence without all the attorneys who get murderers off."

"The idea just blossomed from there," James added. "Then I met Cindy in a support group and it came to life. Dr. Thornton and Beth built the prototype of the skeleton, I worked on the mechanics and developed the skin. Cindy developed the computer that operates Nestor."

Tom turned toward Beth. "Why build an android? Did you really believe you could replace the justice system? It's not that I don't agree, but how did you expect to convince anyone to embrace an android?"

Cindy lifted her head from the table. "Well, gorgeous eyes, my father was murdered and the law did nothing." She laid her head back down.

"I'm sorry," Beth glanced down at her hands. "We all have similar stories."

James chimed in. "I was engaged, and a gang of idiots broke into the Savings and Loan where my fiancé worked. They killed five employees." His face turned red. "They got sent to juvey because they were all underage. Now they're all on the streets."

Tom snuck at look at Beth. "Did you also lose someone?"

"My sister." She swiped her cheek. "She was my baby sister. A serial killer tortured her for days before he cut her up in pieces and buried her. He still had her head, along with several other women's. The courts gave him life instead of death when he agreed to tell them a name and the location of her body." She took a deep breath.

Tom reached out and touched her hand. "You don't have to go any further." He peered at the diamond cross around her neck. "Sorry."

She reached up and caressed the cross. "I gave it to my sister. She never took it off."

"How did you get it back?"

"She was kidnapped from her car. It appeared the killer hit her car to get her off the road. Her cross was under the seat." She sighed loudly. "I'm sure she knew what was going to happen and pulled it off and stuck it under the seat. She always said it would come back to me one day."

"I'm so sorry."

"It's okay. The murderer gives the FBI one name a year. Tells them where the rest of the body is. He wants to make sure they can never execute him. He's up to seven young women now."

Cindy peeked from under her hair and looked at Tom's hand still resting on Beth's. "Nice," she muttered and closed her eyes.

Tom pulled his hand away. "I'm sorry about the loss of your sister."

James took a sip from his cold cup of coffee. "We all lost our loved ones, yet the murderers have not paid. How could we not want justice? Nestor seemed to be the most effective way."

"I understand. I think some of us have been assigned by God to fight evil, but it's never easy to look it in the face. Tell me more about how Nestor works." Tom pushed his stale coffee away.

CHAPTER SEVEN

Flashing lights of several police cars lit the streets in front of the Capitol. With the death of the Senator all of Washington was in an uproar. Though initial reports indicated a natural death, witnesses expressed concern over the strange young man who shook the Senator's hand just before his death.

"Nestor." Not far from the scene, Nestor cocked his head. With the damaged wires almost repaired, he listened intently. "Nestor. Leave the area immediately."

At a slightly faster pace, Nestor strode away from the downtown area. He walked west over the bridge and crossed the Potomac River. Hours later, he entered a less desirable area of Arlington, Virginia. Shadows lengthened across the city as he searched for a place to regenerate.

"Nestor, please respond." Nestor dipped his head.

"Thank you." The voice whispered in his head. "Please turn on your visual receptors so I may see where you are."

Nestor shook his head until the visual pathway to the speaker connected.

"Thank you. Now I want you to respond only to me or Ariel. You are to remain disengaged with anyone else. Do you understand?"

Nestor nodded.

"Good. Please retrieve the key sewn into the lining of your coat before we talk next. Now it appears you still need to regenerate to be at maximum power. Please find a safe place. I will contact you in the morning and you will proceed with your assignment."

Nestor walked until he found a mall. Along the side of the mall, he searched for a location where he could regenerate.

"Hey, man. You lookin for a good time?"

Nestor turned to see a Black man in a leather jacket pushing a young girl toward him. The young black girl moved forward tentatively. Dressed in a tube top and a short, black skirt, she shivered as a light rain fell.

"Brand new stuff, man. Fifty bucks and she's yours. Not even been kissed. You know what I sayin'?" The man reached out and touched Nestor's jacket. Even without skin-to-skin contact, Nestor felt it. "*Wrong.*"

The black man's heavy gold chains clinked as he pushed the girl forward. Nestor tilted his head to the side and regarded the man's eyes. "*Wrong.*"

"Don't like dark meat? Got some white meat too." The man turned toward a black SUV parked a short distance away. "Sugar, get your ass over here."

A petite blond stepped climbed out of the car and approached them. Dressed in a sheer camisole, she tottered on four-inch heels toward the others.

"Daddy," the blond whined. "I thought it was Lovey's turn."

Daddy flung out his hand hitting Sugar across the mouth. "Don't you ever sass me, girl."

Unstable already with the high heels, Sugar fell to her knees. The black girl, peeked a glance at Nestor, fear in her eyes. Cautiously, she approached Sugar and helped her to her feet. Blood dripped down Sugar's skinned knees.

"Whatcha waiting for, man. Damn man, seventy bucks and you can have both the whores."

Nestor delved into the man's memories. Many of the visions fit the *wrong* category but were not punishable by death. Then he saw it. A young girl, beaten beyond recognition. Nestor closed his eyes to escape the vision of the girl.

Nestor allowed the pimp's memories to expand in his mind and then spill out toward the man. The pimp's body started to vibrate. His teeth chattered loudly. Both girls stepped back. Daddy's eyes bulged. He moved backward until his back was against a brick wall. Standing back, Nestor watched as the pimp slammed the back of his braided head against the hard surface again and again. His mouth opened to scream. Instead, only a gurgle escaped his contorted lips. He slid down, leaving a dark smear on the bricks behind him.

Both girls screamed.

Nestor studied the two girls huddled together and shivering in the cold rain. He was confused. The word "*right*" did not totally fit them, but they did not elicit the word "*wrong*." Nestor delved into their minds. His thesaurus began to search for additional words. *Victim* seemed most appropriate.

The blond moved back. She clutched at the black girl. The black girl stood rooted to the spot and stared at Nestor. His mind connected with Lovey. She raised her head and gazed into his gray eyes. He gazed back, nodded, then turned and walked south.

Sugar pulled at Lovey, digging her nails into her arm. Lovey calmly pulled Sugar's hand from her and turned.

"Let's wait in the car."

"Wait? Wait for what? We need to get out of here."

Lovey placed a hand on Sugar's shoulder. "No, we will wait" with that she led the shaken girl to the SUV and both climbed into the back.

After traveling south, Nestor went around a building and ended on the north side of the scene hidden behind some bushes. He stood in the shadows and watched the scene. A squad car approached and a man in a jogging suit ran toward the car. He held his hands up, holding his cellphone high. "I called you," he yelled.

The officer got out of his car and approached the man one hand on his holster. There was an animated conversation and the runner pointed south of the scene. The officer pushed the button on his radio and spoke rapidly. He motioned the man to stay back and went to check out the body lying next to the brick building. Nestor watched as the police officer checked for a pulse, shook his head and again spoke into his radio.

A few minutes later another squad car drove up. Nestor watched as a female police officer approached the first patrolman and then went to the SUV. She pulled out her revolver and called to the two young girls in the black car. Minutes later she led them to her car and placed them in the back.

Nestor watched as an unmarked sedan arrived and a man in a suit jumped out. He went over to the body and checked it out. A van arrived and two technicians got out. They also checked the body. A tarp was placed over the pimp. Nestor felt nothing coming from the figure on the ground. "*Good.*"

The man in the suit spoke to the excited witness, waving his arms and describing the scene. He pointed south. Nestor, now on the north side, watched from behind some bushes. The man in the suit spoke to both officers and then approached the patrol car with the two girls. Minutes later, he returned to his car, pulled out his cellphone and made a call.

Nestor waited. Another dark SUV drove up. A man in a black raincoat jumped out of the driver's side. Nestor recognized him from the courthouse. The passenger door swung open and Beth stepped out. The man in the raincoat and Beth approached the three people on the sidewalk. Minutes later both raincoat man and Beth went to the patrol car with the two girls huddled in the back seat.

"*Right.*"

"Nes … Nestor, are you there?" the voice called to him. He waited. "Nestor, I'm having problems with your retinal scan again. Please blink your eyes several times. Nestor blinked.

"Better. Please scan the area."

Hidden behind a bush, Nestor shook his head from side to side.

"I don't even want to know. Oh my God, what is Beth doing there?"

Nestor watched as Beth squatted in front of the open back door of the patrol car.

"Nestor, you need to get out of there and get regeneration time. Leave now."

Nestor moved away, keeping in the shadows.

"Faster, Nestor. You cannot afford to get caught yet."

The sun was hitting the tops of the taller buildings when Nestor found himself in another part of the city. His internal computer was still processing the encounter with the trafficker and the young girls. Not that he understood this relationship. The thesaurus inside him processed words that came with the image of the girls. "*Wrong*" was vague and did not seem to fit. But "*right*" did not fit either. He was confused. He sensed words like "*weak, victim, good.*" He shook his head and turned down another dark street. A man approached Nestor,. The man's face was hidden under the hood of his sweatshirt.

"Give me your money." The man held out a knife.

Nestor considered him, confused. He cocked his head, trying to get a read.

"Hey, asshole, give me the money." He poked at Nestor with the knife.

Nestor cocked his head again. *"Wrong"*. More words were coming through. *Bad. Evil.* He started to reach for the man.

"You crazy, man. I said give me the money. You want to die?" He poked Nestor in the stomach.

Nestor did not react. Instead, he reached out and touched the man.

"You asked for it," the man yelled at Nestor and stabbed him several times in quick succession.

Nestor ignored the stabbing to his torso and took in the images of several killings. He then redirected the images back to the thief.

The thief's eyes grew large and he turned his knife toward himself. He stepped back from Nestor and screamed as he plunged the knife into his own belly over and over. Nestor cocked his head and watched. *"Wrong. Bad. Evil."* Finally, the man fell to the ground. He was dead.

The rain stopped. Nestor examined his chest and watched as the visible cuts healed. He left the scene. He knew police would show up soon and he must find a place to complete the regeneration.

"Oh, Nestor. Not again." The voice whispered in his head.

With no need for food or rest, Nestor continued to walk. "*Right. Right. Wrong.*" Visuals of these words swirled around in his head.

CHAPTER EIGHT

"We've been searching for hours. I think it's time to call it a night."

Beth peered through the windshield as the wipers whipped back and forth to clear the downpour. "Just a little more."

Tom pulled the car over to the curb and shut off the engine. "Look. We won't find him in this rain. We can go out again tomorrow. Nothing's going to happen tonight."

"I guess you're right. But we both know he had to be responsible for the Senator and that attorney."

"Yes." Tom put his hand on hers, "I guess that confirms the Senator did have something to do with that aide's death in the river. And," he paused as she turned to look at him. "The attorney did a good job of setting up an alibi for his wife's murder. Guess Nestor took care of that for us, too."

Beth dropped her head. "It's all my fault. Why was I so bent on revenge?"

Tom started the car. "Let me take you home." He pulled away from the curb into the storm.

When they arrived in Beth's neighborhood, Tom circled her New England-style condo complex looking for a spot. Rain pelted his car.

"You can just drop me at the front."

"No way." Thunder punctuated his comments. "I'm delivering you to your door."

As he approached the building for a third circuit, lightning lit up the sky and revealed a young man racing toward a car parked in front. Tom pulled up behind him and waited. After a while, the young man started up his car and emptied the spot. Tom looked over at Beth. "See, it never fails. I always find a spot."

"Thank you so much for bringing me home." Beth reached for the door, but Tom stopped her.

"A gentleman never lets a woman walk in the rain." He reached into the back seat and pulled out an umbrella. He got out of the car and opened the umbrella and walked around to open the passenger side door.

"My lady."

Beth laughed and walked close to Tom through the downpour. When they got to her door, she hesitated. "Would you like to come in for a cup of coffee?"

Tom nodded and followed Beth into her condo.

Beth went into the kitchen and was pouring coffee when Tom's phone buzzed and he answered.

"Hello?"

Beth came out of the kitchen, two mugs of steaming liquid in her hands.

"We need to go. There was an incident. Nestor may be involved." He shrugged back into his damp jacket. "Oh, and one of the witnesses asked for you specifically."

"What? Give me a little time to change clothes and I'll be right with you." She left the room, and true to her word returned quickly. She was now wearing jeans, a heavy sweater and boots. Her still-damp hair was now in a bun. She grabbed her coat. "Let's go."

CHAPTER NINE

Both Tom and Beth jumped from the car and approached a group of three. The group consisted of a police officer in a yellow slicker and cap, a man in an overcoat and a short man in a wet jogging suit and hoodie. A tarp-covered corpse lay next to a brick wall.

The man in the overcoat turned as Tom and Beth walked up. "Hey, Tom. Sorry to call you out on a night like this, but I think this might be related to that missing persons case you're working on."

"What do you have, Chris?"

FBI Agent Chris Stephens turned toward the man in the jogging suit. "This is Mr. Rodriguez. He was out jogging when he turned the corner and saw the entire event. He said the victim approach a man with blond hair who was wearing a tweed jacket. It appeared like the black guy," pointing to the body on the ground. "was trying to sell a girl. There were two girls. A black girl and a blonde." He pointed to the car. "There in the black car."

Mr. Rodriguez waved his arms again. "Yeah, I didn't really see the white guy hit the guy, but he must have. The black guy hit the blonde girl and she fell to the ground. Both girls then ran back to the car. The black guy was yelling but the white guy never said a word. Then the black guy just flew backwards and hit the wall. I could hear it from all the way over there." He pointed down the street. "I must have been watching the girls get back into the car. They had to be freezing. They were practically naked. But I heard the guy hit the wall."

Tom turned to Chris. "Mind if I ask a question?"

"Sure, go ahead."

"Did you see where the white guy went?"

Mr. Rodriguez kept looking over at the body on the ground. "Sure. He went that way. Didn't seem to be in a real hurry though." He pointed east.

Agent Stephens interrupted. "A patrol car has already gone looking. Nothing found so far."

"Do you mind if we talk to the girls?" Beth asked.

"No problem. One of the girls even asked for you by name." Chris motioned to the female officer standing next to the patrol car attempting to keep dry. "Mr. Rodriguez, thank you for your input. Will you be available later?"

"Sure." The man in the wet jogging suit pointed to the officer in the yellow slicker. "I already gave my information to the officer."

"Thank you." Tom took out his business card and handed it to the witness. "Here's my card if you remember anything else."

The rain stopped as the two FBI agents and Beth approached the patrol car. The officer opened the door and asked the two girls to step out.

Beth gasped when she saw the two girls. In the dim light, she could see that both girls couldn't be more than fifteen. Before Beth could say anything, the black girl stepped forward.

"You're Beth, aren't you?"

Beth's eyes darkened, then she recovered. "How do you know who I am?"

"He told me." The girl shivered.

Beth turned toward the officer. "Do you have something they can cover up with?"

The female officer nodded and went to the back of the patrol car. While the officer rummaged in the trunk, Beth studied the two girls. "Who told you what?"

"The man who killed Daddy."

"What's your name?"

"I'm Lovey and this is Sugar." She pointed to the blond.

Tom moved closer as Beth asked the questions.

"Tell me about the man. What did he look like?"

Both girls took the blankets offered by the officer and snuggled into them. Sugar jutted out her chin defiantly. "He was a white guy, wearing old man's clothes. Daddy tried to sell Lovey, but he didn't seem interested. Not into girls, I guess." She glared at Lovey. "And he didn't talk to you. He was some kind of mute or something."

Lovey turned back to Beth. "He did too. He told me you would come and you would take care of us."

"Did not." Sugar countered.

"Did too."

Tom touched Sugar on the arm. "Hey, Sugar. Why don't you come over to my car and get warm while these two talk."

Sugar smiled up at Tom and let the blanket fall to reveal an under developed chest. He reached over and draped the blanket around her. He took her elbow and led her to his car.

CHAPTER TEN

Nestor searched for a place to regenerate. His clothes were soaked from the rain. Both his jacket and shirt had been sliced. He wandered about until he came to a large building. Lights spilled through the stained-glass windows which created designs on the concrete. He moved toward it and noticed a cross on top of a steeple. He scanned his database and recognized this as a church. "*Refuge.*"

Nestor climbed the steps and tried the front door. It opened. He went in. The church was empty. He found a seat at the rear of the church and sat down. Rain dripped down the side of his face. He brushed it from his eyes and inspected a life-size statue of a man hanging from a large cross. The cross stood above a table with an ornate cloth on it. He gazed at the figure, confused. "*Wrong. Right.*"

He continued to look up and several words floated through his head.

"Son. Are you okay?"

Nestor turned to see a frail hand on his shoulder. It was a small hand with soft, delicate fingers. He focused on the concerned face of an elderly woman dressed all in black. Her face was old and wrinkled, but her sky-blue eyes radiated youth.

"Do you need help?"

Nestor tilted his head. More words swirled around his data base. *Right. Good. Blessed. Holy.* Many were the same terms he received as he observed the statue. He didn't understand. But he was aware he needed to finish his regeneration. He inspected her eyes.

"Come." She put out her hand.

At her touch, Nestor found his head filled with terms. They churned around and comforted him. He rose and followed her through the church and down some stairs. She led him to a room with piles of clothes on several tables.

"Pick out some clean clothes and you can rest when done." she pointed to a cot in the corner.

Nestor considered her but did not move. She took his hand and placed it on the clothing. He finally nodded. She left the room.

"Nestor? Where are you?" He heard the familiar voice speaking in his head. "Turn on your receiver."

Nestor complied.

"Clothing? Please stand in front of a mirror."

Nestor found a mirror and waited.

"Trouble last night?"

Nestor's head bobbed.

"Okay. Let me assist you in picking out some clothes, but don't forget to keep the key in your jacket. I assume it is still there?"

Nestor nodded.

"Now you will need to go to the bus station. I have left identification and money in a locker for you. I have completed my research and found your first mission. Get changed. You can rest in the church to complete your repairs. Out for now." The voice faded away.

When dressed, he found a cot in the corner and lay down. He closed his eyes and started his final regeneration. Hours later, there was a knock on the door. The nun peeked inside and when she saw Nestor sitting up, she entered. She was followed by a man, also wearing a long, black outfit.

"Son, this is Father Michael."

The priest put out his hand and Nestor allowed him to take his hand in his. Once more, Nestor was flooded with new words and images. He nodded to them both.

"Are you lost, young man?"

Nestor shook his head.

"Are you hungry?"

Nestor shook his head and pointed to the door. The two moved aside and watched as Nestor opened the door and walked out. They followed him through the vestibule. When he reached the main exit, the nun stopped him. "Wait." She disappeared inside. In a few minutes, she and handed him a paper bag. "When you do get hungry."

Nestor moved forward and touched each one of them on the shoulder. He dipped his head slightly, then turned and walked away.

"May God bless you and keep you safe, my son." The priest called to him. He then turned to the nun. "Sister, did you feel what I felt?"

"I felt something but I'm not sure what. I just felt so good when he touched me. It was as if he had blessed us."

They watched as Nestor walked into the park across the street. He stopped when he came to a man sleeping on a bench. He put the paper sack next to the man and walked away.

CHAPTER ELEVEN

Tom blinked the morning from his eyes, confused. A soft purple chenille blanket covered him to his chin. His shoes were thrown on the floor. He rubbed his tongue across his teeth and squinted in disgust. It was then he noticed the aromas of coffee and bacon. He sat up.

"Good morning, sleepyhead."

Tom turned his head. Beth stood holding a steaming mug of coffee. Her red hair hung down past her shoulders. Prisms of light danced around her head as a soft breeze from an overhead fan moved her hair and reflected rays from a window behind her. He inhaled.

"I'm so sorry. I didn't mean to fall asleep."

She walked toward him and handed him the hot cup. "Don't worry about it. We only talked until three. I've got breakfast started. Are you hungry?"

"Yes, but I need to shower and brush my teeth."

Before he could continue, she turned and took a pile of towels off the table. A new toothbrush and razor sat on top. "Go ahead and take a shower in the spare bathroom. It will make you feel better."

He hesitated and then took the stack of towels. "Thank you."

Tom took his time and enjoyed the hot shower while castigating himself. *You shouldn't be here. But I want to.* His desire to know more about Beth won out and he put on a smile, along with his wrinkled suit, and found the kitchen.

"Sorry I fell asleep. Guess I drank too much wine." His stomach growled in anticipation when he saw the table filled with plates of eggs, bacon and toast. "Didn't know I was so hungry."

Beth served him a large plate of food. "More coffee?"

"That'd be great." He held out his mug and waited while she poured. "So last night you told me more about how your team got together to create Nestor. What I don't understand is Dr. Thornton's role. You told me he had no murders in his family."

"Yes, that's true. But he and his wife were very close to my sister. She was his star pupil."

"You then followed in her footsteps?"

"I guess you could say that. After she was murdered, I felt compelled to finish what she started. She wanted to build robotic arms for soldiers who lost limbs. So...."

"Where's the killer?"

"David Ramirez? He's in Texas. But, like I said last night, he'll never really pay for his crimes. He enjoys prison too much. He's a celebrity now and plays your agency like a fine-tuned violin. Oh, I'm sorry." She stood and took her plate to the sink. He picked up his and followed.

"It's okay. I totally understand. Sometimes the law gets in the way of justice." He put his hand on her shoulder. She turned and melted into his arms. He held her. "When this is over…" He took his arms from around her and stepped back.

"I'm …" she hesitated. "It's just so frustrating. He gets to tell where one body is buried every year to avoid the death penalty. It may be years before we know where my sister is."

"I'm here for you." He said and moved toward her. He leaned down and kissed her. "But we'll wait for now."

She smiled up at him.

"Tell me about Cindy. I know about James fiancé, but Cindy didn't say a lot."

"Before I tell you about Cindy, I should let you know the boys that raped and killed James fiancé never got prosecuted. Some legal technicality and their age. One was only fourteen at the time. So, you can understand why James joined the team. Cindy came from New York. She doesn't talk about it, but I do know that her parents were killed in a robbery. They owned a little store in Chinatown. She joined us after she met James in a support group. She is the AI person." Then added, "Artificial intelligence. She built the computer that operates Nestor."

Tom's jumped when his cellphone buzzed. "Excuse me." He went into the living room. When he returned, concern covered his face. "There's been a killing over in Arlington not far from where the trafficker was killed. It that might be nothing, but it could be Nestor. Do you want to come?"

"Of course, give me ten minutes to change."

"Okay, as long as you let me stop by my house to change clothes."

CHAPTER TWELVE

"Nestor, it is time for your assignment. Please go to a store window so I can see you." The familiar voice floated through the air. "Unfortunately, you will have to go back to Washington."

Nestor moved past empty stores in a commercial area of Manassas, Virginia. Lease signs covered several windows. Trash littered the sidewalks. He stood in front of a window with graffiti covering much of it and opened his eyes wide.

"Good. Be sure to keep the shades on. Ugh, I mean sunglasses. And keep the cap pulled low. You only have one assignment and then we will get you out of there. You need to be careful in D.C. Your destination is Columbia Heights. Go to the UPS store on Morton. Your Box number is 2566. Use your key and you will find everything you need. You won't get there till tomorrow, so be careful."

Nestor walked away from the storefront and headed north.

"Nestor don't walk too fast and stay out of trouble. I'll contact you tomorrow morning and find out where you are." Nestor heard a yawn and his head went silent.

At ten the following morning, Nestor walked into the Mailbox store in Columbia Heights. As directed, he went to the box and used the key. Inside, he found a small fanny pack. He removed it from the box, hugged it to his chest. He then pushed through the glass door into the cold morning air.

The voice called to him in a hushed and hurried tone. "Nestor? Can't talk long. Did you find the stuff?"

Nestor nodded.

"Okay. Good. You now have an ID, cash and a debit card."

Nestor opened the fanny-pack and removed several items.

"The debit card is for your assignment after this one. You also have a ticket you will need for later. For now, pull out the little yellow envelope. I'll wait."

Nestor took the small envelope from the pack and tore it open. Inside were three photos of young, dark-skinned boys.

"On the back of the photos you will find the address for those young men. They are very wrong, Nestor. You must complete your task. But wait till dark. You should have no problem finding them out on the street. Be careful. It's a bad area and I want you to focus on those people only and get out of there. When you are done, then you can contact me." The voice went silent.

With hours to spare, Nestor walked until he came to the Church of Christ on Park Road. He walked up the steps and tried the door. It opened. He peeked inside and entered. The church was quiet. He sat on a well-worn wooden bench and closed his eyes.

"Well, hello young man."

Nestor opened his eyes to see a rotund, gray haired man standing in front of him. Large yellowish teeth filled the man's smile.

"You're early for our evening service, but more than welcome." The man wore a dark blue suit with no tie. He reached out his hand to Nestor. "Pastor Lawson."

Nestor nodded and searched the man's mind. *Right.* He then pointed at his mouth and shook his head.

"Oh, sorry. Didn't know you couldn't talk." The Pastor reached for Nestor's hand again and shook it vigorously. "Feel free to stay and enjoy the service. People should be arriving anytime now. I need to set up, so I'll leave you alone for now." Pastor Lawson smiled again and walked away.

Nestor watched as the Pastor set papers out on the chairs. He surveyed the church. A cross hung from an overhead beam just above the pulpit, but the man with the beard did not hang from it. Voices sounded behind him and chattering people entered the church and sat down. Many of the people smiled at him and said "Hello." Nestor sat and watched as the group grew to about thirty.

The pastor stood and welcomed everyone. "I would also like to welcome our young guest sitting in the back. He doesn't appear to speak, but we should all pray for him."

Heads turned and several parishioners smiled and nodded at Nestor. Nestor was filled with words. *Right. Good. Blessings.*

Nestor listened to the Pastor for several minutes and watched as people stood and began to sing. He enjoyed the sound of the music. The music swelled and a sense of *Wrong* entered his head. He turned to see a young man sitting in the very last pew. His head drooped and his entire body sagged.

"Brother Wilson. Welcome home." Pastor Lawson came down the aisle.

The entire congregation stopped singing and turned to look at Wilson.

Nestor sorted through the murmurs of support and zeroed in on Wilson. While he continued to see the word '*Wrong,*' something stronger took over. *Grief. Pain. Loneliness. Guilt.* Nestor delved into Wilson's mind.

In his mind, Nestor watched as Wilson kissed his young son. His wife put the four-year old boy on the ground to hug her husband and wish him goodbye. Wilson kissed his wife one last time then jumped into his truck and backed out of the driveway. The thump and the screams of his wife brought his happiness to an end. He jumped from his truck, grabbed his young boy's body and got back into his truck. "It'll be faster if I take him to the hospital. You wait here."

Shocked, his wife watched in horror as Wilson sped toward the hospital. Finally, she ran back into the house, got her keys and ran to her own car. She headed toward the hospital. With tears blurring her vision, she missed the red light and never saw the delivery truck that hit her on the driver's side. She was dead before the first responders arrived at the scene.

Still sitting on the bench, Nestor left Wilson's mind and watched as several people, including Pastor Lawson, approached Wilson and placed their hands on him.

Pastor Lawson prayed. "Jesus, comfort this man in his hour of need and give him the strength to go on for his young daughter."

Wilson began to weep. Nestor quietly rose and approached the group. He placed a hand on Wilson's head. Others moved back.

Wilson stopped sobbing and glanced up at Nestor. Suddenly, his body convulsed. His limbs trembled. Finally, he stopped twitching and slumped forward. The group around them stood idly, confused. Nestor removed his hand from Wilson then quietly slipped out the door and headed to his assignment.

Fifteen minutes later Nestor stood in front of a large apartment building. He watched and waited. The three young men he was looking for exited the building and headed north. Nestor followed. When they ducked into a dark alley, he was right behind them.

The two older boys appeared to be in their late teens, while the third boy was at least two years younger. When they stopped and took out cigarettes, Nestor approached.

"What ya want, whitey?" One of the older boys demanded. "You popo?"

"We ain't done nothin. Ya better stop hasslin us." The other older boy stuck out his chest defiantly.

Nestor stopped a few feet away and connected with them. *Wrong. Wrong.* He saw the three boys break into a savings and loan and attack the people inside. The attack was vicious. He watched as the two older boys rape a women and then murder all the people in the Savings and Loan office. During the attack, one of the older boys handed a gun to the youngest boy and demanded he shoot the woman he had just raped. Nestor saw the young boy cowering and attempting to move away. The older boy grabbed him and pulled him toward the woman. The woman knelt on the floor and begged for her life. The younger boy took the gun. His body tensed. He fired to the right, missing the woman. The older boy grabbed the gun and shot the woman in the head.

Nestor scanned the three boys and shook his head. He transferred his visions back to the two older boys and watched as they writhed in pain as they felt the pain of being raped and shot. Both boys succumbed to their own evil deeds. The younger boy stood rooted to the spot, too terrified to move.

When the older boys were dead, Nestor reached out and touched the younger boy. The boy screamed and fell to the ground.

Nestor nodded, then turned and headed north. *Right.*

Behind him, the young boy lay trembling on the ground.

CHAPTER THIRTEEN

Beth picked up her cellphone on the second ring. "Hello?"

"Beth, it's Tom." He paused for several seconds. "There's been another attack."

"Nestor?"

"Might be. We need to talk." He waited. "I need your whole team."

"Oh? What's going on?"

"I'll tell you when I see you. Can we do it in an hour?"

Beth paused. "Let's make it two."

Two hours later, Beth ushered Tom into the laboratory conference room. James wore his usual white lab coat and conservative bow tie. He leaned forward expectantly. Cindy slouched in her chair at the far side of the table. She raised her head and peered through her large glasses.

"Hey, Feeb. How goes it?" Cindy said then lowered her head and ignored everyone.

Tom addressed Beth and James. "There were two deaths in Manassas that could involve Nestor."

James focused on Tom. "How do you know?"

"First let me tell you about the case."

Beth waited. "Sure."

Tom sat back. "There were two young men killed. A Rashad Williams and Joe S. Washington. A third boy, Demondre Williams, survived and is talking to the police." He paused and looked at James. "Do any of these names sound familiar?"

James shook his head. "Should they?"

"They were the boys involved in the murder of your fiancéé." He gazed intently at James.

"We were never told the names. Because they were juveniles. You don't suspect me, do you?" James said.

"We need to check every avenue. But, how could you not know their names? Wasn't there a trial?"

James shook his head. "No. Their attorney's cut a deal and the evidence was apparently tainted." James sighed. "Even if I had known their names, what could I do?"

"Wait a minute," Beth stood up. "I thought you said Nestor could be involved . How would you know that?"

"Demondre, the young man who survived, is singing like a bird to the FBI. Said an angel with blond hair took him to hell and let him see what lay ahead if he continued this path. He said God told him to tell the entire truth."

"What does that mean?"

"His brother, Rashad, and Joe did the killings. They tried to force Demondre to kill a female, but he chickened out. He was only thirteen at the time. It was a gang initiation and Demondre's already given the FBI the names of the gang members who ordered the murders. Rashad lied to the gang and told them Demondre had participated. He did it to protect his little brother." Tom turned back to James. "I'm sorry, James, that your fiancéé was killed as a gang initiation."

James nodded. "But I don't understand why you think this was Nestor or that we had anything to do with it."

"Demondre described his 'angel.' Also, there was a woman at her window across the street who saw everything. She couldn't say it was Nestor, but she did say it was a white man with a hoodie. She said the white man didn't even touch the two young men when they fell to the ground. He touched Demondre and left him on the sidewalk. She went to the boys after the white man left and found Demondre curled in the fetal position on the ground. The other two boys were dead. He kept asking God to forgive him." Tom said to James. "Are you sure you didn't program Nestor to get revenge?"

James let out a lungful of air. "I swear. I didn't even know their names. I only built the body, not the AI."

"I know, the Artificial Intelligence." Tom looked over at Cindy, who was now staring at him.

"Don't look at me, brown eyes. I didn't even know about the gang kids. Sounds to me like you got a rogue android." She put her head back down on the table.

"I wish we could be of more help," Beth offered. "Nestor was programmed only to read minds he has contact with and then carry out punishment. Are you sure it was him? It just sounds impossible that he could find the kids who committed those murders two years ago."

"We need more to go on to find him. If it was him, we have a major problem. I've already contacted the Director to see about notifying all our offices."

CHAPTER FOURTEEN

While Tom was meeting with Beth and her team, Nestor arrived on a Greyhound bus at the Port Authority Terminal in New York City. He stepped off the bus and found the waiting area. The five-hour trip allowed him time to regenerate and he took in the stimuli around him.

After a while, a person, huddled into an oversized hooded overcoat, sat down next to him. He tilted his head and inspected her. She looked familiar, but her hair was different.

"Hello, Nestor. I'm Ariel."

He nodded. This voice was different, but similar to the one he was programmed to respond to.

"Follow me. We've got a lot to do."

Nestor stood and followed the young Asian woman out of the terminal.

Ariel led Nestor down several streets then boarded a bus. They traveled several blocks, got off and walked until they came to an industrial complex. Ariel went to a large unit and entered a code on the keypad and opened the door.

"Here we are Nestor. This will be your home for a while." She reached inside and flipped a switch, bathing the large room in fluorescent light. About one quarter of the large room was filled with lab equipment, tables and computers. In the center of this area sat a hospital bed.

Once inside, she turned to the android. "Nestor, I want you to take your clothes off and lie on the bed." She pointed and watched as he went over to the bed and removed his jacket and shirt. When he started on his pants, she smiled.

"Nestor, you have to take off your shoes before your pants."

Nestor sat on the bed and took off his shoes. He then got up and removed the remainder of his clothing. He lay back on the bed, face up.

Ariel inspected his body. Nestor turned his head toward the door as if listening. Ariel turned and watched as the door opened. A short figure clad in a large overcoat with hood entered. Gloved hands reached up and lowered the hood to reveal a head of shoulder length black hair. The visitor raised her head and smiled.

"Hey, Ari. How goes it?"

"Finally. I thought you would never get here." Ariel moved forward and threw her arms around her sister. The two girls hugged and jumped up and down. "Welcome home, Cindy."

"We've done it! What do you think?" Ariel's sister shrugged out of her coat and threw it on a chair. Together the two moved to Nestor, lying on the bed.

Nestor studied the two young women. *Same. Duplicate. Twins.*

The new arrival put on a lab coat and approached Nestor. "Nice, huh?"

Ariel laughed. "Very nice." She glanced at his groin area. "Too bad."

Together they laughed until they cried.

Nestor listened to the voices. *Same voices. Creators. Bosses.*

Cindy leaned forward and studied his eyes. "Time to power down, Nestor."

Nestor closed his eyes. All appearances of life disappeared and he became limp.

"What did you just do?" Ariel asked.

"I completely shut him down. Now we will be able to work on his features. If he were still active, he would heal as soon as we made a change."

"How will you turn him back on? If he can't hear you, what will you do?"

"You'll see. Now let's get started. Do you have the tint?"

Ariel nodded and retrieved a bottle of yellowish-brown liquid.

"You can start swabbing his skin. I'll start on his face."

While dabbing the tint onto Nestor's skin, Ariel watched her sister slit Nestor's eyes and put a filler into his eyelids. Cindy then made several other slits and changed the shape of his cheeks. "Are you going to sew him up?"

"No. When we wake him up, his skin will heal." She then made a cut at the base of the nose and lifted the skin. Ariel heard the sound of scraping as Cindy shaved down the tip of the nose. "I'm done. How about you?"

Ariel stepped back. "Okay, now what?"

"We finish his hair and then we wake him up." She cut off his scalp and all his hair and then placed a new head of hair over his skull.

Ariel's sister stopped before pushing a button behind Nestor's ear. "You know what? Let's just let Nestor relax for a while. I've been cooped up in the crazy DC nest of cuckoos for two years. I want to have some fun."

"Yeah, baby." Ariel did a little dance. "Bye, bye sweet prince. See ya in a few hours. Come on, sis."

Cindy followed her sister up the stairs to a spacious loft. She twirled around taking in the entire living space. Then she ran to the first door of two separate areas. "Ugh. This must be your bedroom, clothes all over the place."

Ariel's lower lip protruded. "Don't be a pain, sis. I've been putting all this together by myself while you were living the high life in DC."

"Some life." Cindy wandered over to the second bedroom. "You try living like a friggin nerd for two years." She stopped at the door. "Lavender. My favorite. Thanks." She paused, went to her sister and kissed her on the cheek. "What about clothes?"

Ariel strolled toward a smaller room and opened the sliding door. "Voila! Two of everything." This room was a large walk-in closet with clothing hanging on racks. Purses, accessories and shoes were arrayed on shelves.

Cindy smiled. "Let's do it."

An hour later, the twins left the loft dressed in identical silver lame dresses and stiletto heels. Their glossy, black hair was piled on top of their heads.

The Uber driver snaked through the downtown area and finally deposited them in front of a nightclub, music pulsing.

Cindy pushed her way through the crowd and deposited a wad of bills into the bouncer's hand. He glanced down quickly and ushered the girls past the red rope. Groans and complaints followed them into the club.

At the bar, Cindy ordered two Shirley Temples. The bartender scowled when he handed her change. She responded by leaving a dime. "Up yours."

As both girls enjoyed the thump of the music. Cindy felt a hand caress her behind. She turned, her hand sliced sideways through the air, hitting a young Asian male in the throat. He dropped to his knees, tears clouded his eyes. He coughed. She lifted her foot to kick him when Ariel pulled her back.

"You a racist? Don't like guys from the Mainland?"

Cindy's eyes turned into narrow slits. "Don't like creeps feeling me up."

"You, b…." He placed his hands on the floor to push himself up.

Ariel's stiletto came down hard on his hand. He yelled and reached for Ariel's leg. She stepped aside, grasped Cindy's arm. "Let's get out of here."

The twins ran from the club, laughing. They jumped into the first Uber waiting at the curb and headed home.

Instead of going up to the loft, Cindy went directly to the lab. Ariel followed.

"Cin, you shouldn't have done that. We can't afford to let people know who we are."

"My dear sister," Cindy said in an English accent. "I will not abide a Chinaman feeling me up solely because I am from an island. Did that poor excuse of a man think he had the right to put his hands on the arse of a Japanese female?"

"Seriously, Cindy. Our parents did everything they could to keep us away from the criminal life." Ariel waved her arms in a wide arc. "I know all of this is the result of drugs and money laundering, but at least we need to thank our father for putting us in schools under other names."

"I know, I know. And I would give all this up just to have our mother back. If it hadn't been for her, we wouldn't be here tonight."

Ariel lowered her head. A single drop of liquid ran down her cheek. "If it hadn't been for you and mother ... If she hadn't pushed us behind that screen when they came ... If you hadn't turned me away when they killed her." She stopped.

Cindy went to her sister and took her in her arms. "That is why we are doing what we are doing. Our father's money helped me create Nestor and now he can help us make things right."

Still clinging to her sister, Ariel sighed. "Yeah. You're right."

Cindy pulled away and went over to Nestor. "Watch this."

Fascinated, Ariel regarded her sister pulled Nestor's ear forward. She then reached in and flipped a small switch. Slowly, Nestor began to stir. First his fingers twitched, then his toes, then all four limbs. Finally, he opened his eyes. Ariel stood mesmerized.

"Wow, that is amazing. I can't believe you did this."

"I had help." She paused. "Nestor sit up."

"That reminds me. What happened to your team?"

"After Nestor disappeared, the hospital shut down our lab and fired all of us." She gasped. "Of course, I left right away. James is moving to Arizona to work with the VA on prosthetics for wounded veterans. I think Beth is in love." She laughed. "The FBI guy is really sexy. Got some great golden eyes." She handed Nestor some new clothes. "Enough about them. I'm sorry for what I had to do, but they'll thank me in the end."

Nestor finished putting on his clothing and stood before the two women.

Ariel shook her head. "No one will recognize him. Great work we did before going out and dealing with idiots."

Her sister nodded. "Now we can get justice for our parents."

"And Beth will see what we can do once we take care of her situation."

Cindy studied the new Nestor. He was now a five-foot seven-inch Japanese male with short black hair. "Okay, my Nestor. It is time for your next assignment."

"Cindy, I'm exhausted. Can't we get some sleep?"

"Sure. Nestor you can relax tonight and we'll see you in a few hours."

"Don't you have to shut him down again?"

"No, he'll be fine. Let's get some shut-eye."

Dressed in a silk Kimono, Cindy stepped into the lab to see Ariel already hard at work. Nestor sat on the table facing away from Cindy.

"What time is it?" she yawned loudly.

Nestor turned at the sound of her voice, revealing two large cavities where his eyes should have been.

"Whoa. What the hell?"

Ariel turned with a small tray holding two eyeballs. "We forgot to change the color. But I made some improvements. Come. See."

Cindy cinched her robe and moved forward. Like a skilled surgeon, Ariel connected several wires and reconnected Nestor's eyes, now dark brown in color. Cindy remained quiet.

With Nestor's eyes in place, Ariel turned toward her sister. "Now watch." She pulled out her cellphone and handed it to Cindy. "Hit the eyeball app."

Cindy tapped the phone and immediately a view of the lab came up.

"Okay, Nestor, do your stuff." Ariel smiled at her sister.

Nestor swept his head from side to side, scanning the entire lab. He was even able to focus in on small objects.

"This is so cool, sis." Cindy kissed her sister on the forehead. "You are the greatest. You improved his visual capabilities."

"Then let's get started on his new project."

"Actually, Ari, last night gave me a great idea."

"What do you mean?"

"Did you happen to notice the tat on the Chinaman's neck?"

"Not really."

Cindy moved over to a computer and pulled up some photos. "Look at these."

"Yeah?"

"It's the Triads."

"Triads?"

"The Triads are the Chinese version of the Yakusa."

"You mean like Father's gang?"

"Yes. So, let me tell you my idea."

CHAPTER FIFTEEN

At five that evening Tom pounded on the lab door. James opened it. James hadn't shaved and his lab coat was smudged and coated with dust. A t-shirt announcing "God Bless America" replaced his usual neatly-pressed shirt and bow tie.

"How'd you get in?" James asked and turned back to putting files into cardboard boxes.

"I'm FBI. Where's Beth."

"I'll get her." James left the room.

Beth entered through the same door carrying two large boxes. Tom hurried over and took the top box from her arms. He set the box on a table and turned back as she set down the other box. Her long red hair was tied up with a worn shoelace. Several strands hung down the side of her face. Smudges of dust covered her cheeks.

He felt a longing and turned away. "Have you seen it?"

"Seen what? I have no idea what you're talking about."

"Nestor. He's back in the city. Where's the rest of your team?" Tom dropped into a chair.

"Cindy's gone and we're packing."

"What? Why are you packing? Where's Cindy?" Tom jumped up.

"After you left, we received word the project is cancelled. We are no longer employees of Geolab."

"I don't understand. We still need to find Nestor."

Beth sat down. "You'll have to do it on your own. We've all been fired. Guess we made the company look bad."

Tom sat down across from her. "I'm sorry."

James came back into the room. He barely glanced at Tom. "All packed. I'm heading home."

"Wait. I came to show you something. Do you have a laptop?"

"Of course," James replied. "I'll get it." He left the room and returned a few minutes later with his computer and set it on the table.

"Can you sign into YouTube for me?" Tom asked.

Both James and Beth glanced at him.

"Why?" James asked.

"Just indulge me."

Tom pulled up the video he was looking for. "Watch this."

A shaky cellphone video showed someone who appeared to be Nestor touching a man sitting on what appeared to be a church pew. Several people stood around and gasped as the man shook and finally passed out.

"Oh, my God. It is Nestor. He's killing someone in a church." Beth covered her mouth.

"Wait, there's more." Tom shushed them.

In the next scene, the man on the floor rose and stood before the camera, his eyes filled, but he smiled.

"It's a miracle. Both my wife and my son are in heaven. I saw them." The man proclaimed.

Another man entered the scene. "I'm Pastor Lawson. We were visited by an angel today." He hugged the other man. "The healing has begun." The video ended.

"I don't understand," James said. "What did Nestor do?"

"I'm not sure, but we need to go to that church. It may be the only way we can find Nestor." Tom stood.

"You don't understand. We don't have jobs anymore." Beth got up slowly.

"I don't care about the company," Tom said to them both. "I need you. By the way, where is Cindy."

"When we got the news, she took her personal belongings and left. We don't even know where she went." Beth explained.

"Doesn't matter. Are you ready to go with me?"

After packing up the rest of their belongings, James and Beth put their stuff in their cars while Tom waited.

"You go ahead, I'll finish up here." James hugged Beth and headed back to the office.

After fighting evening traffic, they arrived at the church. It was almost six. Beth got out of the car and waited for Tom. "We should have called."

Tom took her by the elbow and led her toward the church. "I think they have an evening service. Come on."

They found Pastor Lawson sitting at his desk in a tiny office at the back of the church. He was working on his sermon for the upcoming service. He stood when Tom peeked in the door.

"Hello? Can I help you?" He reached out a large meaty hand and shook Tom's.

"I'm Special Agent Tom Ford of the FBI and this is Dr. Beth Middleton. We would like to ask you a few questions about the incident on Sunday that was posted on YouTube."

"Have a seat." Pastor Lawson sat down. "You must mean the mute gentleman. I must tell you, if I had ever doubted Jesus, after that my faith is stronger than ever."

"I don't understand." Beth leaned forward

"Well, the video taken only showed the effect on Wilson. You know, the seizure. But there was a lot more. You'd have to talk to Wilson to understand." The pastor glanced at his watch. "In fact, he should be coming in any minute."

A door slammed in the vestibule. "Kayla, wait for me," a voice called. The office door opened and a little girl of about six ran into the room. Cornsilk braids swung back and forth as she took in the group. "Hi, Pastor. We're here to help."

Seconds later the door opened again and a young man peered in. "Excuse me, Pastor. Kayla, you shouldn't just run in without knocking."

"Wilson. Come on in. I want you to meet some people." Pastor Lawson stood, as did Tom and Beth.

They shook hands and all sat down. Immediately, Kayla climbed up into Beth's lap. "Hi. What's your name?"

"I'm Beth and I'll bet you're Kayla."

Pastor Lawson came around the desk. "Kayla, how about you and I start putting out the choir books?"

Kayla jumped down from Beth's lap. "Bye," she said and followed the pastor out of the room.

Wilson started to get up.

"Mr. Wilson," Tom began.

"Just Wilson."

"Sorry. We are checking on a missing young man and wanted to ask you about the incident last Sunday."

Wilson raised his eyebrows. "Did he do something wrong?"

"Oh, no." Beth shook her head. "His family is looking for him. He doesn't speak and they are very concerned about him."

Tom leaned forward. "Can you tell us what happened?"

Wilson glanced up as if saying a quick prayer. Then he looked directly at Tom. "I was in a bad way. Just lost my little boy and wife on the same day. I really didn't want to go on. I'd taken Kayla to her grandmother's for the day and had it all planned out. Came here to ask God why."

Beth sucked in air but held it together.

Tom nodded slowly. "I'm so sorry."

"No. Don't be. That young man saved my life."

Beth glanced over at Tom and frowned. She said nothing.

"How, if I may ask." Tom asked.

"I killed my baby son and my wife," he blurted out. Tom stiffened.

"My precious baby boy ran under the wheel of the truck." Wilson breathed deeply. "I tried to get him to the hospital in time. I was too late." He eyed Beth. "I told my wife to stay home. She didn't listen. She took Kayla over to the neighbor's, got into her car and was speeding to the hospital. They told me she never even saw the truck that hit her."

Beth shifted in her chair, but Tom touched her arm lightly. She sat back.

"That was over a month ago. I had a hard time at the funeral. I didn't want to continue. Didn't think I had a right to live after that." Wilson stared at them, then dropped his head and studied the floor. "I had it all planned it out on how I would kill myself. I was going to take the truck and make it look like an accident. Then with insurance, Kayla would be taken care of." He stopped and looked up. "I came here that Sunday to yell at God for taking my family and then blame him for my actions."

"I'm so sorry, Wilson." Beth's eyes were wet.

"It's okay." He paused. "Like I said. I had it all ready. Then Pastor Lawson noticed me and came and laid his hand on me. So did others. But I felt only one hand. It was like hot, yet cold. I didn't know who was touching me. Then I felt pain and anguish. I saw it all happen over again. It hurt so bad." Wilson sobbed. Beth and Tom restrained themselves from showing any reaction. "Through the pain I saw it."

"What?" Both said at once.

"I saw my family. They stood in a light. My wife was smiling and holding my little boy in her arms. She was happy." Wilson closed his eyes, as if seeing them again. "They were beautiful. She smiled at me and my boy waved. She mouthed something."

Beth moved forward slightly.

"She said 'I love you.' I knew she was okay and she was waiting for me. Then she said, 'Take care of Kayla.'" The light faded and they were gone. I no longer felt the pain. I felt love. I felt peace. The hand left my body and it was like it took all the pain with it. Then people were picking me up off the floor. I didn't even know I'd fallen." Wilson stopped. He smiled broadly. "I know. You probably want me to tell you if that hand belonged to the man you are looking for." He shrugged. "I don't know, he stood behind me and I never saw him."

Just then, Pastor Lawson stuck his head in the door. "Everything alright?"

Tom stood. He moved to Wilson and offered his hand. "It was such a pleasure to meet you and I wish you all the best of luck."

Beth got up and hugged him Wilson. "Take care of that beautiful daughter."

"Pastor Lawson, I have one more question. Did you see the young man?" Tom asked. "If so, can you describe him?"

"Well, yes, Agent. Average height, light hair, light gray eyes. That's about all I remember. As you can guess, things were a little busy here. Didn't even see the young man leave. Sorry."

"That's okay, Pastor. Thank you for your time."

Back in Tom's car, Beth let out a sob. "How is any of this possible? Androids don't have feelings. How, how, how?" She put her face into her hands.

Tom leaned over and took her in his arms. "Hey. This isn't your fault."

She closed her eyes, still safe in his embrace. "How can it not be my fault? I'm one of his creators." Her stomach growled.

"You sound hungry. Let's go get something to eat. It's after six."

"I'm fine. I'm not hungry."

"Your abdomen begs to differ and I'm hungry. So don't argue with me." He released her, reached into the glove compartment and handed her a tissue. "I know a great place."

The sun was almost gone when they pulled into the parking lot of a small Italian restaurant nestled between a beauty salon and an electronics store. Tom ran around to open the door and ushered her into the dimly lit eatery. It smelled of garlic and red wine. Almost immediately after entering, a beautiful blond hurried forward and threw her arms around Tom.

"It's been more than a month. Where have you been?"

Beth looked away.

Tom kissed the blond on the cheek and hugged her tightly. "Melissa, I want you to meet a friend." He turned to Beth. "This is Dr. Beth Middleton. Beth, this is my baby sister."

Melissa turned and threw her arms around Beth's neck. "Welcome to our restaurant. I'm making something special tonight. It's a meal I came up with but I think it will taste great. I hope you two will be my tasters. Been working on it for a while, just to get it right. Think it will go great with a nice Chardonnay. I hope you're okay with chicken." Without waiting for a reply, Melissa continued. "Mario should be here soon. Went to go get the baby." With that, Melissa turned on her heels and left.

Beth gawked at Tom.

"Don't worry about my sister. She's a tornado. Imagine growing up with that." Tom laughed. "Come on." He led her to a back table. "This is the family table. It has a view of the door but still provides some quiet."

Tom seated Beth, stepped away and returned to set her place. "Hold on. I'll be right back." He disappeared into a back room. In less than five minutes, he returned with a bottle of wine and two glasses. "One of the best white wines. I hope you like it."

"It'll be fine." Beth took a sip of the pale liquid. "Can any of this really be happening?"

"What do you mean?"

"Nestor is basically just a machine. Yes, he has a computer running him, but he is not a human. That could not have been him." Frustration filled her voice. "But it was, wasn't it?"

"It certainly looks that way. I hate to say this, but we need to look at your team."

Beth peered up her eyes rimmed in red. "It couldn't be James or I, we worked on the mechanics. We're both Mechanical and Electrical Engineers, not Software Specialists. Besides, James is probably gone. He was leaving tonight. He took a job at the VA in Phoenix." She exhaled. "In fact, he said they would love me to come work there too."

Tom let out a sign and she examined his face. "I haven't said yes."

"Good." He placed his hand over hers. "Not yet. Please. What about Cindy?"

"Cindy? I tried calling her. No answer."

"What do you know about her?"

"Just that Bill, oh, Dr. Thornton, brought her in. He told us her parents were murdered several years ago. I don't know much else. Kind of strange. Dr. Thornton gave her the highest compliments. Ph.D. in Computer Science, Medical degree in neurosurgery, etc. I know she's smart, but you saw her." She hesitated. "Dr. Thornton was the one who mostly interfaced with her. She did all the programming."

"Could she have done more?"

"Like what? Nestor's just a machine, albeit a smart one. He was only supposed to access the memories and display them on the screen and then send them back into the mind of a murderer. Nothing else. Oh, my God. What have I done?"

Tom took Beth's hand. "Beth, it'll be okay."

The sound of a toy trumpet interrupted their conversation. They turned toward the clatter and a little girl of about four marched up to them tooting her horn. The girl had a curly mop of red hair and bright blue eyes. She wore a tiny apron, stained with tomato sauce. Right on the little girl's heels was a young boy about two years older. He also had the bright red hair. He carried a basket of freshly-baked bread. Beth salivated when he set the basket on the table. The parade wasn't over yet. Next, another girl of about eight years old stepped up with a large salad. She placed the bowl on the table and curtsied.

"Hi, I'm Ruth." The girl smiled. "Are you dating my uncle?"

Beth reddened. Before she could answer, Tom cut in.

"Hey Ruthie, you know better than to ask personal questions."

The six-year-old stepped forward. A large gap filled his smile where his two front teeth were missing. "I don't ask personal questions. I'm Micah." He stuck his hand toward Beth.

Not to be outdone, the youngest elbowed her brother out of the way. "I'm Ester and I'm four years old." She held up four fingers.

Beth laughed. "Hello to all of you." She shook Micah's still outstretched hand."

Ester climbed into Tom's lap. "Are you going to take me to the zoo?" she asked, putting her chubby arms tightly around his neck.

"All right, you guys. Back to work." Melissa stood holding two large dishes. She set them on the table and helped Ester get down from Tom's lap. "Sorry," she said to Beth and Tom. Then to the children. "Dad will be here in a minute. Go take off your aprons and get ready."

"I'm here," a husky voice called out. "I'm here."

Beth tilted her head up. A very tall man, probably about six foot five, stood smiling down at the group. He had black hair and matching eyes and carried a toddler identical to Ester on his hip. He turned to Beth and smiled, large dimples cratering his cheeks.

"Hi. I'm Mario. You must be Beth. Tom has talked about you."

Beth peered at Tom. He grinned like a Cheshire cat. Beth quickly glanced away.

"Okay everyone, time to let these people eat. The two dishes I brought out are a light shrimp fettuccini with green peppercorn sauce and chicken and eggplant in a brown butter sauce." Melissa and Mario gathered their children. "Antonio, the manager will help you with anything else. We're going home to put these young ones to bed." With that the entire clan disappeared.

"This food looks delicious. I've never heard of either." Beth leaned forward to take in the aromas.

Tom reached across the table and began serving. "Melissa is quite the chef. She started cooking when she was about eight and never stopped. Mom just decided to let her cook and off she went. Meeting Mario was a match made in heaven. He was working for an international chef and moved to Washington, D.C. to cook in one of the new restaurants. It was just a matter of time before they opened their own restaurant." He set a loaded plate in front of Beth.

"You expect me to eat all that?" She giggled. Then she took a bite of the eggplant and chicken mixture. "Yum. Maybe I will eat all this. It's delicious."

They ate, drank wine and talked about their lives. Finally, Beth scanned the restaurant. "Oh my, we are the only ones in here. What time is it?"

He pulled out his phone. "It's almost ten."

Just then Antonio peeked around a corner. "Mr. Tom, will there be anything else?"

"No, Antonio. Just the check."

"Oh, no Mr. Tom. Your sister will not let me give you a check." He started clearing empty dishes.

Beth yawned. "I'm sorry. It's been a long day."

"All right, let's get you home." Tom stood and pulled a hundred dollars from his wallet and placed it on the table.

"Isn't that a large tip?"

"No, Antonio will only take out what is fair and write up a receipt for another patron. We do this all the time."

A short while later Tom walked Beth to her condo door. He turned her toward him and kissed her lightly on the lips. "Can I ask you something?"

"Yes."

"Don't make a decision to leave or take that job in Arizona. I want to check on something first."

"I may not have a choice."

"Just promise me you'll wait."

"Okay."

He turned and started to walk away. "I'll call you tomorrow."

She opened the door and went in. As soon as she reached the living area, she fell back on the couch and then softly rubbed her finger over her lips and smiled.

CHAPTER SIXTEEN

Sunlight broke through the frosted windows of the loft and Cindy opened her eyes. She threw off the covers and dropped her feet onto the cold concrete floor. Her bare feet searched until she found the warm bunny slippers. Cranes and cherry blossoms decorated a bright red kimono still lying at the foot of the bed. She shrugged into it and shuffled into the bathroom. Her mouth tasted like sour cranberry juice. Darn mocktails. Teeth brushed and face washed, she bundled her silky black hair into a bun and used a comb to hold it in place. Then she went to get her sister out of bed.

Ariel was not in her bedroom and the bed was undisturbed. Cindy made her way to the open kitchen and brewed a pot of tea. She placed the teapot, cups and scones on a silver tray and went down to the lab. The cups rattled as she stepped on the stairs. Sure enough, Ariel perched precariously on a stool. Her head lay on her arm and a small puddle of drool glistened on the cold metal table. She snored softly.

Nestor sat on a table near Ariel, facing away from Cindy. Cindy placed the tray on a polished metal table nearby. Nestor turned quickly to face Cindy.

She jumped back upon seeing only voids where his eyes should have been. She bumped the edge of the tray with her hip. The tray slid across the smooth surface. Tea, China cups and scones crashed to the floor. Ariel, jolted awake, fell off the stool and landed hard on her rear end. The silver dress slid above her thighs. Her face matched the color of her red panties as she attempted to cover herself.

"What the heck?" Ariel pulled herself up from the floor and smoothed down her silver dress. "Good thing I wasn't still wearing my stilettos. I could have stabbed myself." She shook out her hair and wiped saliva from her mouth.

Cindy eyed her sister. "Where are Nestor's eyes?" She placed her hands on her hips.

"Don't blow a gasket. I upgraded them."

"Upgraded them? What are you talking about? He was fine."

"Calm down. I know you don't think I have your scientific skills but while you were off in D.C. programming him, I was doing some learning on my own."

Cindy snorted. "I'm sorry. I didn't mean to imply you weren't capable."

"Okay." Ariel turned to the table and removed a small glass box. She popped the lid open and held it out to Cindy.

Cindy picked up the two orbs and scrutinized them. "They look the same to me except the color is a darker. What's different about them?" She handed back the box.

"Just watch." Ariel turned to Nestor. "Nestor lie down."

Ariel pulled over a step stool and climbed up. She worked for about five minutes then hopped down. "Voila."

Cindy moved closer to Nestor. "So?"

Ariel picked up a cellphone from the table near the computer and handed it to Cindy. An Icon blinked and she tapped it. Once the app was open, she saw the lab. "We already know we can see what he sees."

"Okay, smartie. Watch this." Ariel turned back to Nestor. "Nestor, do your stuff."

Nestor examined the room. Cindy followed his gaze with the phone. The movement stopped then started again.

"Cool. So he can actually stop action?"

"Be patient. There's more."

Cindy continued to watch as the cameras in Nestor's eyes stopped action and zoomed in close to a bottle in a cabinet across the room. She could read the label. "Good job, sis."

"Still more, silly." Ariel grinned. "Nestor. Play back."

Cindy watched as the entire new video played from the beginning. "Aren't we missing video while he is playing back?"

"Not at all. He can record with one eye while playing back with the other."

"Okay. But what about storage? Do we have to back up everything on the Cloud?"

Ariel shook her head. "Not at all. I gave him twelve terabytes of storage. He can video for years and never run out. Besides, I don't think we want this information out on the cloud, so I have it blocked so it won't go there." She turned to Nestor. "Okay, Nestor. Take a break." Ariel puffed out her small chest and beamed. "Now you can start working on what we talked about last night. I'm going to go take a shower. Dancing all night really takes it out of you." She picked up her high heels, went over to the mess of broken cups and spilled tea, picked up a scone and stuffed it into her mouth. "Ta, ta."

Cindy watched her sister leave, then walked over to a table cluttered with computers and other electronics. For several minutes she searched websites until she found what she was looking for. "Nestor, this one's gonna be hard. I want you to read all these sites I've opened for you and then we begin our next stage." She led Nestor to the computers and showed him what to study. "I'll be back in a while."

Nestor connected to the computer and began the scan.

Two hours later, both sisters returned to the lab. They were dressed in identical outfits of blue jeans and turtleneck sweaters. They found Nestor lying on a steel table, his legs bent at the knees and swinging back and forth. The girls glanced at each other with eyes wide.

"How do we know he digested all the websites you pulled up?" Ariel asked.

Cindy shrugged. "Since you upgraded the camera, let's see what the playback shows."

"Nestor, start playback from two hours ago." Ariel tapped on an icon on the desktop computer and together the girls watched as Nestor showed a playback of the information on the Yakuza, Japanese gangs prominent in Little Tokyo and throughout New York. "Stop. Stop."

"What?"

Ariel turned to her sister. "Have him go back a couple of tabs." Ariel watched the screen intently. "There. Why was he watching research on Chinese gangs?" There on the computer was an article about the Triad, a vicious Chinese gang. "What does the Triad have to do with Japanese gangs? They didn't kill our parents. Someone in Yakuza did."

"Think about it." Cindy tilted her head to one side. "What if we let the gangs fight it out and Nestor just has to stir the pot?"

The girls sneaked a peek at Nestor.

"Oh. Then there wouldn't be any question of how they were killed." Ariel turned to Cindy. "How should we dress him?"

Cindy went to a corner and retrieved a bag and pulled out some well-worn clothing and showed them to Ariel.

Ariel went through the old shirts and two pairs of worn jeans. "Why old clothes?"

Cindy went over to the computer and pulled up some photos of Yakuza gang members. "See the clothes these guys wear. Lot's of gang type clothing.

We can't have Nestor look like a wanna be. At least not yet. He's just going to watch and record. Then we'll figure out how to get him into the gang."

The sisters helped Nestor get into his new, old clothes and provided him a worn, but heavy jacket with a hood.

Ariel stepped back. "Sorry about the heavy jacket, Nestor. But it's cold outside and even though you can't feel the weather, it would look weird if you went outside underdressed."

"Nestor, time to do some reconnaissance." Cindy took charge. "We need you to watch and record." She stepped up to him and investigated his face. "Do not pass judgment. I don't care if you find guilty people." She paused. "Do not pass judgment. Not yet. Do you understand?"

Nestor nodded and allowed the sisters to lead him to the door and send him on his way.

CHAPTER SEVENTEEN

"**What's to think** about?" James pleaded. "Don't you want to get away from the whole Nestor thing?"

"Yes and no." Beth breathed deeply and tucked the phone under her ear. "James, I think I'm in love." She took a sip from a steaming mug of tea.

"What? You think? Who?"

Beth paused for several seconds. "Agent Ford, Tom."

"Like I couldn't have guessed that. I saw how you glanced at him. Have you told him?"

"I'm not sure how he feels. Maybe our relationship is only based on finding Nestor. But, if I move to Phoenix, I'll never know."

"Hey. I understand. You can get a job anywhere. I'm sure the VA in DC would love to have you. I can call my friend if you'd like."

"Not just yet. Tom got approval from the Attorney General to keep me on as a consultant with the Agency to find Nestor."

"Have you heard anything about Nestor?"

"Not since we saw the video at the church and the death of those teens."

James snorted.

"Oh, I'm sorry, James. But at least they know you didn't have anything to do with those killings. It must have been just coincidence that Nestor ran into those kids."

"Yes, Agent Ford called and told me I wasn't a suspect." James hesitated. "Have you found Cindy?"

"Not yet. It's like she fell off the face of the earth."

"Could she have had anything to do with what Nestor did?"

"Cindy? Really? I know she's a genius but come on. Cindy's only good with computers. She's a mess when it comes to dealing with people."

"Just saying. Dr. Thornton brought her in. We don't even know if her parents were really killed."

From the living room a doorbell chimed.

"James, I need to go. I think Tom is here. We have a meeting to go to."

"Okay, Beth. If you ever need me, you know I'm here for you. Love you."

Beth hung up the phone and hurried toward the door.

CHAPTER EIGHTEEN

The twins spent the morning cleaning up the loft and straightening the lab. After a light lunch, Cindy sat down at the computer. She tapped the Icon for NEST and waited. Nothing happened. "Ariel," she shrieked, "I can't find Nestor."

Ariel hurried over and searched through the files. "Well, he did record something. Look."

Cindy watched as Nestor entered a Japanese restaurant in Little Tokyo. Several young men attired in identical t-shirts and headbands watched as Nestor came in and sat at a table nearby. When the server brought a menu, Nestor pointed at an item and sat back. A young man with the head of a dragon tattooed on his bare shoulder approached Nestor.

"Whacha doing in here?" The young man demanded.

Nestor gazed up at him.

The young man glared at Nestor. He put his hand on Nestor's forearm. "I asked you something, man. Answer me."

Nestor's eyes closed. Cindy knew he was taking in the memories of the man touching him. "Do not pass judgement," she whispered to herself.

Cindy and Ariel waited. Nestor opened his eyes but did not look directly into the eyes of the aggressor. He lowered his head and motioned to his mouth.

The gang member shoved Nestor. "Can't talk, huh. Well, this ain't no place for you. So get out."

Nestor nodded and kept his head low as he slid out of the chair and left the restaurant. He moved into a doorway across from the restaurant and watched until the group came out and headed up the street. Pulling up his hoodie, Nestor followed the four men. When they went into an apartment building not far away, Nestor scanned the address and left the area. The girls watched as Nestor wandered about the city until he came to another building with a Star of David on a small sign in front.

"Isn't that a Jewish synagogue?" Ariel asked. Cindy nodded. "Why did he go there?"

"I don't know, sis." Cindy grabbed a microphone and spoke to Nestor. "Nestor you need to come home now."

Nestor either didn't hear or ignored Cindy's voice and went into the Synagogue.

"Nestor, come home now."

Nestor went into the synagogue and sat on a pew and scrutinized his surroundings. He studied the carvings and strange letters in front of him. He did not move. He closed his eyes and the girls lost contact.

"What is he doing?" Ariel asked.
"I don't know."

Nestor's eyes opened and the wrinkled face of an old man came into view. Nestor turned his head from side to side studying the long gray beard and cloudy eyes. He looked down as the man reached out and placed his hand on Nestor's arm. A faded tattoo was visibly seen on the man's lower arm.

"I'm Rabbi Cahn," the man introduced himself. "Can I help you, young man?"

Nestor blinked several times and squeezed his eyes shut. The camera feed stopped.

"Oh, my God," Ariel exclaimed. "He's not going to hurt that old man, is he."

"How would I know? That's where the camera stopped recording." Cindy stammered. She examined the computer, but the screen remained blank.

CHAPTER NINETEEN

Nestor peered into the face of the Rabbi. Visions beyond anything he had ever seen filled his head. He blinked several times at the sights before him and then shut off the camera feed. He watched as hundreds of emaciated people; men, women and children, were herded into rooms and gases were pumped in. The people screamed and clawed, trying to find a way out. They all died. Nestor watched as men in uniforms lined up people and shot them. The soldiers then pushed their bleeding bodies into pits. He contemplated the horrors until he found the memories of Rabbi Cahn. Rabbi Cahn was young, probably about ten years of age. He reached from a cage as they took his mother into a room. He listened to her screams as they tortured her.

Nestor tried to shut it out, but the visions were too intense. He heard the young Cahn call out to God to save them. Then Nestor watched as Cahn covered his ears to the screams and sank down to the floor of the cage. Only then, did the sound of gunfire interrupt the visions of death. Men in khaki-colored, dirty clothes entered the camp. The Nazis in the camp either ran or dropped to the ground. Screams were heard from every corner. Nestor watched as an American soldier yanked open the cage and pulled young Cahn out. He cradled him in his arms and carried him to a truck. Young Cahn pointed to the building where his mother had stopped screaming. Another American solder raced to the building and kicked open the door. Shots rang out. Minutes later, the solder exited. He carried Cahn's battered mother out. Her dress was torn and covered with blood but she clung to the soldier. Cahn raised his eyes to the heavens. "Thank you, God."

Nestor put his hand on Rabbi Cahn's arm and studied his eyes. Rabbi Cahn smiled and nodded. Nothing more needed to be said.

Nestor left the synagogue and headed back to the lab.

CHAPTER TWENTY

Nestor's camera came back online almost two hours later. Ariel, who was now watching the screen, yelped. "He's back."

Cindy raced to the computer. "Where is he now?"

"Looks like he's almost home."

Both girls ran to the warehouse door and investigated the street. Nestor, head up, walked toward them.

"Nestor, not good." Cindy chided him as he entered. "Where have you been? What did you do to that old man? Why did you turn off your camera? How did you turn off the camera?"

Nestor ignored both girls and went over to a chair and sat.

Ariel eyeballed him, then turned to Cindy. "You know he can only answer yes or no questions."

Cindy hesitated. "You're right," then more slowly. "Nestor, did you hurt that old man."

Nestor sat impassively. His face, as usual, showed no emotion or response.

"Gee, I wish you guys had put some emotion on that face." Ariel sidled closer to Nestor. "He looks so stoic."

Cindy turned away and went to a computer. "I had nothing to do with the structure, only the programming. And, how would they give an android emotion?"

Ariel screamed. "There's something in his sweatshirt."

Cindy whirled around and watched as the front of his hoodie moved. Nestor unzipped the front and a small head peeked out.

Ariel screamed again. "Oh my God, what is that?"

Cindy moved closer. Large golden eyes peered up at her from a soft furry face.

Ariel inspected the strange creature. "It looks like a Moglin, you know, a Gremlin. Those things that multiply when they get wet."

The little animal stepped out further.

"It's a cat." Cindy offered.

"But why is its face so flat? Looks like someone smashed it. And where's its fur?"

Cindy took the small, peach-colored cat from Nestor's lap and lifted it into the air. It emitted a weak meow. "It's a Persian cat. Looks like someone tried to shave it and nicked it in several spots. Poor kitty." She picked up the cat and cradled it in her arms.

"He's so little. How do you think Nestor got him?"

"Don't know. Why would he bring a cat home?" Cindy placed the cat on a metal table and stroked his thin, shaved body. The cat began to purr.

"He'll need some food." Ariel reached out and tentatively touched the small animal. It purred louder. "Look how bony he is."

Behind them, Nestor stood and went over to a desk. He picked up a yellow pad and pen. He walked to Ariel and tapped her on the shoulder. She turned and he handed her the pad.

Ariel shrieked and the cat jumped off the table and hid.

"What now?" Cindy inquired. She turned and saw Ariel holding a yellow pad, her hand shaking.

Ariel thrust the pad to Cindy. "Look."

Cindy viewed the pad with MINE written in large block letters. Both girls watched Nestor, eyes wide.

Nestor pointed at the pad and then at the cat cowering under the table.

Cindy searched Nestor's eyes. "Nestor, what are we going to do with a cat? We need to find this poor animal a home."

He shook his head and pointed to the yellow pad. He stomped his foot. The girls turned toward each other then back at Nestor.

"Okay." Cindy shrugged. "I guess we can keep the cat."

Nestor lowered his head, dropped to the floor, gently lifted the cat out from under the table and the cat immediately cuddled into his arms.

"What about food?" Ariel said, "And we'll need a litter box, water and medicine for his cuts."

"We can use a box with shredded paper for litter now and I think we have tuna upstairs. We have plenty of medicine in the lab." Cindy went to a cabinet and pulled out a tube of antiseptic. Nestor approached Ariel and placed the small cat in her arms.

Cindy took over the care of the small cat. Ariel tentatively held him while Cindy applied medication to the several small cuts on his torso. "Looks like someone with no experience shaved off most of his fur. They only left the fur around his face and the pompom at the end of his tail."

"Why would they shave it?"

"Well, it's not summer, so it can't be because of the weather. He must have been all matted." Cindy paused and peeked at his teeth. "Teeth haven't been cleaned in a while, if ever. Hard to say how old he could be. Doesn't look like he's been fed for a while either."

"You sure it's a boy?"

"Yeah, pretty apparent," pointing at his behind.

Ariel blushed and then glanced around. "Hey, where's Nestor."

Footsteps could be heard on the stairs. The girls turned to see Nestor balancing a tray as he stepped into the room. Cindy picked up the cat while Ariel raced over to see what Nestor carried. She took it from him and carried it to Cindy.

"He brought tuna and milk." She gawked at Cindy. "How does he know this stuff?"

"Guess he wants to feed his cat."

Ariel put the tray on the ground and Cindy put the small, cat on the floor in front of it. The cat attacked the tuna with vigor.

"I guess I better get back to work. We need to finish our research on the Yakuza." Cindy went to the computer and pulled up several websites. "Nestor, you can start reading again. I'll put together a litter box for your cat."

Nestor went to the computer and sat down. Cindy took paper from the shredder and spread it on a metal pan while Ariel checked the cat for any more cuts.

"Ow."

Cindy looked up from the litter pan and saw Ariel holding her hand against her chest.

"It scratched me."

Cindy went to her sister and checked out the small scratch. "Baby. This is smaller than a paper cut. Hold him and I'll trim his nails." She retrieved some nail clippers from a drawer and started clipping. The small cat struggled but let Cindy trim his nails. "I better check on Nestor," she said when done with the cat.

Nestor sat in front of the computer, which was now shut off.

"Have you been doing your homework?" Ariel asked.

Nestor ignored her and got up. He went over to the cat and picked it up.

"Hey, what should we name the cat?" Ariel asked.

Nestor retrieved the yellow pad now lying on a table and wrote a message. He turned the pad toward the two girls, NESTOR KITTY ONLY.

Ariel laughed and handed the cat back to Nestor. "I guess NKO could mean Niko. Does that sound right?"

Nestor nodded, picked up the cat and went over to his chair and sat. The cat circled twice and then snuggled into his lap.

Nestor's lip twitched on the right side as he watched the girls go about their business.

CHAPTER TWENTY-ONE

Beth and Agent Tom Ford were ushered into a conference room adjacent to the FBI Director's office. They sat down and waited.

Beth's leg began to shake. She shut her eyes and took in a deep breath. Tom reached over and took her hand.

"Hey, it'll be okay." He whispered.

Beth began to chew on her lip. "Why would they call us in? Do you think they found Nestor?"

Before he could answer, the Director and the Attorney General of the United States walked in. "Coffee?"

Tom and Beth both shook their heads.

"We're fine," Tom offered.

Both men sat down. The AG sat forward and placed his elbows on the table. "I wanted to let you know we have been looking into the Nestor issue." He nodded at Tom. "Agent, thank you for all your hard work in trying to locate the android. The Director and I met recently to determine how best to move forward. We have the full support of the President."

"The President agrees, we must continue to search for the android, but we cannot let the public know of his existence." The Director of the FBI looked at Tom. "Tom, we want you to continue the search and we will provide the necessary support in searching for possible locations."

The AG then looked at Beth. "However, we think there is more that we can do."

"I don't understand," Beth said.

The AG looked over at the Director. "The android, what do you call him? Nestor?"

Beth nodded.

"Well, to put it bluntly, he works."

Tom and Beth looked at each other.

"We checked out both the Senator and the attorney that died were indeed guilty. We have proof the attorney killed his wife and set it up to look like a burglary. While we don't have definitive proof the Senator killed the girl, we did find enough evidence to support a strong motive. So, having Nestor out there is actually benefitting us."

"But aren't we playing God?" Beth asked.

The Director smiled. "Isn't that what we do anyway? Better we have control over the outcome."

Tom piped in. "But, we don't know where Nestor is."

"And that is why we asked you both in. Not only do we want you to continue searching for him, we want to work on a second android."

Beth's eyes widened. "What?"

"Yes, we would like you to bring your team together and create another android. Of course, with some modifications."

"My team? James and I are the only ones left. We don't even know where Cindy is." She paused.

The Director reached down and pulled a file from his briefcase resting near his chair. "Yes, Cindy. We had the NSA do a search. Of course, they didn't know why." He opened the file and pushed it toward Tom. Beth looked on.

"As you can see, there is no Cindy Takahashi. And she has a twin sister." He took back the file. "We haven't found her yet, but we will."

Beth closed her eyes and leaned back. "I need to think about this."

"I understand," the AG said. "We are not looking to take over the world or go on a hunt for criminals. The purpose would be exactly what you and Dr. Thornton originally planned. But the program would have full support."

The Director spoke up. "Yes, we are not asking you to play God. We just want to fine turn our legal system and make it more effective. But think about it. Tom will continue to lead the search for Nestor and we would like you to come on full time in helping him."

The meeting ended. Tom and Beth left the FBI Headquarters holding hands.

"Let's talk about this when we get home." Tom said.

Beth nodded, but remained quiet.

They had a lot to think about. Not only the search for Nestor but also their wedding plans.

CHAPTER TWENTY-TWO

The girls struggled to get up hours later as the sun streamed in through the loft windows. After both were showered and dressed, they entered the kitchen area in search of food. Dressed in identical blue jeans, white tennis shoes and white woolen sweaters. They bumped fists when they saw each other and simultaneously said "Twinsies."

"Want some eggs?" Cindy asked as she pulled an egg carton from the refrigerator.

"Sure. Can we add some cheese?" Ariel pulled out a block of cheddar cheese. "So what do you think about our new family member?"

Cindy stopped whisking the eggs and contemplated Ariel. "Don't forget we have a mission. We can't be sidetracked thinking we can take care of a pet."

"I know, I know. But until we get to that point, we might as well let Nestor have his cat."

"Okay, but don't get too attached. When we are done here, we move on to Texas."

"Yes, Texas. Don't know how we're going to accomplish that one. Why do we even need to?"

"Ariel. I already told you. Dr. Thornton had a goal when he first put this team together. I promised him I would help him make it happen."

"Okay. You promised. But why didn't he tell the other team members?"

"Beth and James would never have agreed to this. They are both too moralistic."

"And you're not?"

Cindy shaved thin slices of cheese over the eggs and served them on waiting plates. "Of course. Just not as much as them. I, you and I can get the revenge we have always wanted." She handed one plate to Ariel. "Besides, we are ridding the earth of some evil people."

"Should we really play God?"

"Oh, come on, Ariel. We've been planning this for two years. Don't flake out on me now."

"I won't. It's just that Nestor seems to be learning. Why do we have to sacrifice him? I know. I know. It's all part of the plan. I won't bring it up again."

"Finish eating and let's go work with Nestor."

The girls went down the stairs to the laboratory and stopped at the door. Cardboard boxes littered the floor. Some open and other still sealed with brown shipping tape.

"What is this?" Ariel asked.

Amid the boxes, Nestor sat on the floor playing with a plastic rod with feathers across the floor. Niko gave chase. A large cat condo, already assembled, sat nearby. Various other cat toys, a new litter box, cat sand, and food were strewn about.

Ariel scrutinized one of the sealed boxes. She picked up an invoice and handed it to Cindy.

"Oh, no! He spent five hundred dollars on cat items and paid for overnight shipping." Cindy studied the room and saw her wallet sitting next to the computer. "Nestor. You used my credit card."

Ariel approached Nestor. He continued to swing the cat toy back and forth. "Nestor, what did you do? How did you do this?"

The right side of his mouth lifted as he pointed at the cat.

Ariel stepped back. "Cindy, I think he's trying to smile."

"Impossible." She knelt and looked at Nestor. He nodded and again, his lip lifted slightly. "Oh, my." Cindy fell back to the floor, landing on her butt.

"Cindy, what do we do now?"

Nestor put down the toy and stood. He went over to a table and picked up the yellow pad. He wrote on it and turned it toward the two girls. FINISH MISSION.

Still on the floor, Cindy raised her head to him. "You sure?"

Nestor nodded.

"Okay, then let's get this done."

Two hours later, the girls sent Nestor out on his mission.

CHAPTER TWENTY-THREE

Nestor walked into a small Japanese restaurant on the lower East Side and slid into a back booth. The diminutive, wrinkled waitress shuffled over to him and handed him the menu. He quickly pointed at the egg flower soup and sat quietly. When the hot soup was delivered, he nodded and remembered what the twins had taught him. He took the spoon, dunked it into the soup and pretended to blow on it. Nestor spent the next thirty minutes scooping a spoonful of soup and pouring it back into the bowl.

The door to the restaurant opened and three young men entered. The elderly waitress flew past Nestor and scurried toward the back. He did not need to translate to understand her yells.

"Yakuza, Yakuza!"

An old man came running into the restaurant from the back and held a cleaver up high. He stopped just opposite Nestor's table.

One young man stepped forward. "What you gonna do, old man?" He said. Then he calmly pulled a gun from the back of his waistband and pointed it at the chef.

The old man dropped the knife, put his hands out in supplication and stepped back to the old woman. He put his arm around the woman's shoulder and lowered his eyes. "Okay, we pay."

The young man with the gun waved it around. "Of course, you pay." He laughed. Then he looked over at Nestor, calmly pretending to sip his soup. He waved the gun under Nestor's face and smiled. "Look boys, it's the dummy." He then slapped Nestor on the head. "You a wanna be, kid?"

Nestor closed his eyes and searched the minds of the four men. In the mind of the leader, he saw several killings. Most were rival gang members. The pimply-faced teen was equally as bad with at least two murders. Only one had not yet committed a murder but had participated. *"Do not pass judgment."* Nestor remembered Cindy's command and sat back. He put down his spoon, peered at the leader and nodded.

The leader slid into the booth opposite Nestor. "How do we know you're not a cop?"

Nestor tilted his head to the side. He focused on the boy who only participated in a murder and sent him positive messages regarding himself.

The boy turned to the leader. "Hey Kiyoshi, I like him. Can't we just test him and if he passes, we keep him around." Then the boy slid into the booth, crowding Nestor and put his arm around Nestor's shoulder. "I like him."

"Ya, Little Boy, you like everyone. But okay. We'll give him a test." Kiyoshi stared directly in

Nestor's face. "You willing to make a delivery? You do understand, don't you?"

Nestor nodded.

A pimply-faced young man, with elipses tattooed below his right eye, seated next to Kiyoshi piped in. "You going to send him to see Tiny Kong?"

"Yeah, Tiny Kong." Kiyoshi laughed. "Can you run an errand, dummy, without screwing up?"

Again, Nestor nodded.

Kiyoshi pushed the pimply-faced boy out of the booth and glared at Nestor. "Okay, dummy. Let's go."

Nestor placed a twenty-dollar bill on the table as instructed by the twins. As the group got ready to leave, Nestor watched as the pimply-faced man pocketed the twenty, but did nothing and followed the men out.

Nestor followed the men out to the alley behind the restaurant. When they came to large black SUV parked in the alley, Kiyoshi opened the trunk, removed a yellow envelope and wrote on it with a Sharpie. When done, he handed the envelope to Nestor.

"Hey, dummy. You think you can deliver this envelope to the address on the front?"

Nestor nodded and headed out of the alley. He listened to the conversation behind him as he walked away.

"What's in the envelope?" Little Boy asked.

"Just a few hundred dollars I owed Tiny. Mostly, it's a test. I'll still break Dummy's legs if it doesn't get delivered." Kiyoshi paused. "Tiny will probably break his neck for just showing up anyway. If he returns, I guess we can give him some more work."

Pimple-face laughed.

"Come on. I wanna call Tiny and tell him to look out for Dummy."

"You don't want one of us to follow him?" Pimple-face asked.

"Nah. Like I said, he doesn't deliver we find him and break his legs."

CHAPTER TWENTY-FOUR

Nestor walked to the door of a run-down warehouse next to a dive bar. He knocked on the door. A lock slid back and a young boy of about thirteen peered through the crack.

"What you want?"

Nestor pointed to the envelope with the name "Tiny" written in large block letters.

"You wait." The boy shut the door and Nestor heard the lock slide into place.

He stood silently for almost fifteen minutes before he heard soft footsteps coming toward him from the bar. He turned to see the boy who had opened the door in front of him. The boy had greasy black hair and was extremely thin.

"Come." The boy said in a squeaky voice. He turned and headed back toward the bar. Nestor followed. Once inside, the boy pointed to a back table and quickly disappeared.

Two men sat at the table, mostly in shadows. The man facing Nestor stood. He had to be over six foot five and weigh over three hundred pounds. Muscles bulged from his biceps and shoulders. The other man kept facing the wall.

"Who you?" Tiny asked.

Nestor stepped forward and handed Tiny the envelope.

"I asked, who you are?"

Nestor pointed to his mouth and shook his head.

"Ah, so you a dumb mute, huh?"

Nestor nodded. He considered the mind of Tiny. Tiny had not killed anyone but had hurt many people during his life. Then Nestor saw what he had done to the young boy with the greasy hair and many others boys. He pulled his gaze away from Tiny and reached into the mind of the man still sitting at the table. As if sensing the intrusion, the man turned and glared at Nestor. Nestor recorded the face. In this man's mind, Nestor saw what he had been searching for.

Tiny opened the large envelope and pulled out a number ten envelope stuffed with money. He read the note Kiyoshi had written on the inner envelope. "Man you just too stupid to do anything with. Get your ass out of here."

Nestor nodded and walked away.

CHAPTER TWENTY-FIVE

Nestor waited until he was two blocks from the bar to review the camera footage stored in his data bank. He had finally found the murderer of Cindy's and Ariel's parents. He turned off his internal camera and headed home. A figure stepped from an alley and blocked Nestor's path.

"Hey man, you got any blow?" The man was unshaven and had on a well-worn leather jacket and ripped jeans.

Nestor scrutinized the man standing before him then tilted his head.

"Man, I saw you come out of Tiny's. He's the main man. You must have some blow?" The man got closer moved his face to only inches from Nestor's face.

Nestor investigated the man's mind and was surprised. The man was really an undercover police officer and was lying about wanting drugs. He was not a bad man. Nestor shook his head.

The man pulled out his badge. "What is your name?"

Nestor pointed to his mouth and shook his head.

"You're mute?"

Nestor nodded.

"Did you get any drugs from Tiny?"

Nestor shook his head.

"Do you have anything to do with him?"

Nestor shook his head but held out his hand as if handing over something.

The detective moved closer. "You gave him something?"

Nestor nodded.

The man put his hand on the side of his head, sighed and reached into his pocket. He handed a small note pad and pen to Nestor. Nestor took the pad and scribbled: Letter from Kiyoshi.

The detective took it. "You work for Kiyoshi?"

Nestor shook his head.

"You look like a nice kid but Kiyoshi is a bad guy and he will only use you and spit you out."

Nestor nodded.

The man took a card from a back pocket and handed it to Nestor. "Take this and contact me if you find yourself in trouble. My name is Detective Bergman."

Nestor took the card, looked at it, then nodded and handed the card back. He then looked into the mind of the detective. He now knew what he needed to do. He reached out his hand. The surprised detective shook Nestor's hand. Holding the detective's hand confirmed what Nestor needed to do.

Two hours later Nestor knocked on the door of a brownstone in a middle-class neighborhood. A woman in her late twenties opened the door. She wore a bright pink and purple scarf covering her head.

"Can I help you?"

CHAPTER TWENTY-SIX

Shortly after ten that evening, Nestor opened the door to the lab and entered. Cindy and Ariel lay asleep on a mattress with Niko curled up between them. They sported pajamas with fairy tale characters dancing around. Both girls snored softly.

While Nestor stood watching the sleeping girls, Niko opened his coppery eyes and regarded Nestor. He jumped up and ran toward him, waking the girls. Both girls propped themselves up on elbows and watched as Niko ran to Nestor and climbed up his jeans. Once there, he perched on Nestor's shoulder and nuzzled his ear.

Cindy grinned. "Niko must know he can't feel those claws or he just doesn't care."

Nestor scratched Niko's chin and then walked to the computer. He typed for several minutes and then hit enter.

A disembodied voice came out of the speaker. "Found man."

Both girls jumped. Cindy gawked at the screen and turned to Ariel. "He's using the text to sound option. Why didn't we think of that?"

"Found who?" Ariel asked.

"You found him?" Cindy regarded Nestor. "Where?"

"Who did you find?" Ariel insisted.

"Show video." The computer's mechanical voice answered.

"Found who?" Ariel's voice rose.

The video came on and Cindy moved closer. She watched as Nestor spoke to the man with the evil eyes. "That's not him."

Nestor pointed at the mirror above the big man's head.

"Oh, my." Cindy's mouth dropped open.

"Cindy. Tell me." Ariel threw up her arms.

Cindy turned toward her sister. "The man who killed our parents."

"But I thought you didn't see."

Cindy lowered her head and closed her eyes. A single tear made its way down her cheek. "I lied, sis. I covered your eyes but I saw it all."

"Oh. I'm so sorry." Ariel embraced her sister and both girls cried. Ariel sobbed and then focused on the paused video. "He needs to die."

Nestor shook his head.

Cindy gawked at him,. "It's your job Nestor. You need to get revenge."

Again, Nestor shook his head. Niko lifted his head, butted Nestor's cheek and licked his ear. Nestor lifted the fluffy Persian from his shoulder and placed him in his lap. He shook his head and typed into the computer. "He follow orders."

"You have rules, Nestor. You must kill."

Nestor picked up Niko and went over to a cot and lay down. He placed Niko next to him and closed his eyes.

Ariel continued to stare at the video, which continued to play. "Oh my gosh. Cindy. Look at this."

Cindy turned away from Nestor to watch the video. They watched as Nestor met a man on the street. The two men talked for a short time and the other man handed Nestor a card. Nestor then moved away at a fast pace and soon arrived at a small brownstone. Nestor walked up the steps and knocked at the door. A young woman opened the door.

"Can I help you?"

Nestor had the sound turned off, but Cindy could read the woman's lips. She watched in fascination. What was Nestor up to?

Nestor glanced down at the swollen belly and offered his hand. The woman hesitated and then took it.

Light exploded in her head and heat ran through her body. She wanted to scream but the pain went away and was replaced with a pleasant warmth and calm. The woman closed her eyes, gave in to the feelings and collapsed to the floor. Nestor stepped inside, picked up the pregnant woman and placed her on the couch. After placing a pillow under her head, he covered her with a blanket and pulled it to her chin. He then locked the door behind him and headed toward home.

After Nestor placed the woman on the sofa, Cindy turned to face him.

"Nestor," Cindy asked. "What did you do?"

Nestor picked up Niko, sat in front of the computer and typed. "She sick. I fix."

"Nestor, Nestor, Nestor. You can't do that. Now someone can connect you to the healing in DC. Now that you're Japanese, they may connect you to us. Or at least me. We need to finish this fast and move to our next assignment." Cindy got up and paced.

Nestor scooped Niko into his arms, went back to the cot and shut himself down.

"Why is this such a problem?" Ariel asked.

Cindy groaned. "Because he healed a man in DC and it's now on social media. If the FBI hears about another healing, especially Agent Ford, he may figure us out."

"Come on, Cindy. We're all the way in New York. How can he connect this to Nestor?"

"Better safe than sorry. Let's just get ready to end our assignment here and move on."

Ariel nodded. "Okay, I'll get the RV ready."

"Just pack the essentials. We don't need all the clothes and stuff. I'm kind of excited to get this over and start new lives."

"Me, too."

Both girls watched Nestor and the purring cat, shrugged and went about their business.

CHAPTER TWENTY-SEVEN

The plastic soles of Cindy's bunny slippers flapped on the stairs as she made her way to the lab. At the bottom of the steps, she stopped and surveyed the room and saw several boxes were packed and piled on metal tables and numerous propane tanks lined one wall. Nestor entered the lab from the garage, picked up a box and returned to the warehouse, which housed the Volkner luxury motor home. Cindy saw Ariel hunched over the computer, typing furiously.

Cindy shuffled next to Ariel. "Good morning."

Ariel's head swayed slightly. "Sis, what gives? It's two o'clock."

Cindy glanced up at the windows. "But it's light outside."

"Two o'clock in the afternoon."

Cindy groaned and plopped down on a nearby stool. "Oh, dear. We've wasted an entire day."

Ariel waved her hand in the air. "Not so, dear sister. Most of the work is done."

Cindy examined her sister.

"After you went to bed last night, Nestor went out and did a little mind surfing."

"Mind surfing? What are you talking about?"

Ariel put her finger to her lips. "As you know, Nestor does not need to touch everyone to read their minds. So, last night he went into the area where Kiyoshi hangs out and found out about a gun shipment tonight." She whispered. "He might be able to help us find where the killer hides out."

"What's his name?"

"Be patient. First, the gun deal. That is our way of getting rid of Kiyoshi and his crew. Then we set up Tiny for sex trafficking. Finally, we go after Takeo Tsukasa. He is the first lieutenant. He will lead us to the Oyabun, or the family boss." Ariel explained.

"Okay, now you are losing me. How are we going to do all this and get out of town in one piece?"

"Well, my dear sister. As a master hacker, I have all the information I need. First, we set up Kiyoshi and his followers for the gun buy by contacting a wannabe in the Triad who would just love to move up by giving his bosses a tip like this and by taking out the Yakuza."

"And we do that how?"

"Remember that guy who grabbed you at the club?"

Cindy waited. "Yes."

"I found him," Ariel pivoted the computer screen toward Cindy and showed her a mugshot of Sam Wong, complete with booking number.

"Ah, and I suppose you know how to get the information to him?"

"Of course. Just watch." Ariel took out a burner phone and dialed. She waited for several seconds. Finally, Cindy heard a voice answer.

"Is this Sam Wong?" Ariel paused. "I'm the girl who stomped on your hand at the club last week." Ariel moved the phone away from her ear. Cindy could not hear, she guessed there were several unsavory expletives. When the phone became quiet, Ariel put it back to her ear. "Hey, I called to say I'm sorry and I have some information for you." Again, she moved the phone away and waited. "I know. I'm so sorry, but I need your help. It's about the Yakuza."

Cindy motioned for Ariel to turn on the speaker. Ariel shook her head and listened as Sam asked a question.

"Yes, I am Japanese. And, no, I am not part of the Yakuza. I hate them. They killed my parents." She waited. "Look, I really do have information for you. If you can use it, it will help me keep my brother out of trouble with Kiyoshi."

Cindy pointed at the phone. Ariel pushed her away.

"Look, my brother is disabled. If they get their hands on him, they will just abuse him or kill him." She hunched forward. "It's good information. A shipment of guns coming in tonight. A large shipment. Enough to take out the Triad." Ariel smiled at her sister. "I swear to you on my parents grave. Check the manifest at the dock. I'm sure you have people. A large container is arriving from Yokohama. It's listed as furniture. Yes, yes. Berth 89 at nine tonight. Sorry, I don't know the name of the ship."

"I'll check it out." Sam's voice could be heard through the phone.

Ariel hung up the phone and smirked. "One down."

Cindy moved closer to her sister. "Okay, now bring me up to date on the rest. What is mind surfing?"

"Come on. You programmed Nestor. You should be aware of his mind connection abilities."

"Yes, when he comes into contact with people but what is mind surfing?"

Ariel squinted her eyes. "You programmed him. Don't you know?"

Cindy shook her head.

"Mind surfing is when he has previously connected with an individual, he can actually reach their mind from a distance." Ariel turned back to the computer. "In this case, he was able to find out about the gun delivery and some things about Tiny."

Cindy watched her sister.

Ariel continued. "He currently has a stash of trafficking victims in that building next to the bar where we saw Takeo Tsukasa. They are all being transferred tomorrow afternoon. But first, the Oyabun, the leader of the Yakuza. He is meeting with Takeo to select the favorites. Only the best girls are saved for a special group of politicians and celebrities. We can find out who the Oyabun is and stop the entire thing."

"And how are we supposed to do that?"

"Oh, ye of little faith, dear sister Cindy. If we get to the bar by noon, we should be able to finish our business with Takeo and the Oyabun and be on our way before the police raid the place."

Cindy eyeballed the ceiling and sighed loudly.

Ariel smirked. "First, I need to make another call."

"Can I listen in this time?"

"Of course." Ariel picked up the phone and the card Nestor had received from Detective Bergman. She dialed and waited for several rings.

"Yeah?" The detective answered.

"Is this Detective Bergman?"

"Yes?"

"You don't know me, but you gave your card to my brother the other night outside of a bar."

"Your brother? Oh, the young man who didn't talk. He showed up at my house, didn't he?"

"Yes, detective. I have some information but you can't tell anyone about him."

"If your brother had anything to do with what happened to my wife, no one would believe me. Anyway, what information do you have?"

Cindy hesitated.

Ariel shifted the conversation. "How is your wife?"

Bergman paused. "Doctor's called it a miracle. The brain tumor is gone."

"So you think it was my brother?" Ariel waited.

Bergman paused. "Okay, I won't tell anyone about your brother. What do you have?"

Ariel told Bergman about the children in the rundown hotel. "They are transferring the children tomorrow afternoon. If you wait until three," she explained. "you will also be able to arrest some pretty influential buyers."

"Hmmm, I'll check it out."

Ariel hung up the phone. "Now it's time to find out who the Oyuban is and make him pay for our parent's death."

Cindy tilted her head to the side. "How do we do that and survive?"

"You'll see."

Just then, Nestor came in from the garage and picked up another box. He looked at both girls, nodded, and returned to the garage.

CHAPTER TWENTY-EIGHT

Ariel stood at the door with hands on her hips. "Come on."

Cindy pulled back on her dark hoodie and checked Nestor. "Okay. Let me grab my phone."

"No cellphones. They can be tracked. We'll take a burner." Ariel pulled a box off the shelf and grabbed a phone. "Let's go."

Ariel led the trio from the warehouse and down one block. She pulled a key from her pocket and pushed the remote. A black Escalade chirped in the night. "Do you have your gloves on?"

"Yes," Cindy answered. "Where'd you get that car."

"I'll tell you later. Just make sure you have gloves. We can't leave any fingerprints."

Cindy jumped into the front seat after making sure Nestor was buckled into the back.

A block from the port, Ariel hid the car between a building and a large dumpster. "Hurry, we need to get into place before dark."

On the roof of an abandoned warehouse, they waited and watched the shadows lengthen into solid darkness. Cindy and Ariel nibbled on peanut butter sandwiches and waited in silence. A light snow drifted down upon them. Ariel pulled a blanket out of her backpack and the girls cuddled under it. Both shivered as they waited.

Nestor crawled to the girls and lifted the blanket.

"Hey, Nestor, you don't get cold. What are you doing?"

He ignored Ariel and moved in between them. He draped his arms around them and heated his body.

Both girls sighed. "Thanks, buddy." When the lights of several cars entered the port area, Cindy checked her watch. "That must be Sam and his Triad gang. It's almost eight."

The girls pulled out their night vision binoculars and scanned the scene. "Yep, they're hiding their cars behind some containers near Berth 89."

Cindy nodded. "Now we wait for Kiyoshi."

Just before nine, Kiyoshi and his crew drove onto the dock and started loading boxes into a thirty-foot delivery truck. The boxes were unloaded from a ship from Japan. They were almost finished when the Triad members came out of the darkness, dressed like Samurai. Cindy nodded at Nestor. "It's time," she whispered.

Nestor focused on Kiyoshi's mind. Through their binoculars, the girls watched as Kiyoshi pulled his gun and aimed at the leader of the Triad. Even from the roof top, the trio heard the yelling. A member of the Triad jumped forward and shot Kiyoshi. He fell to the ground, unmoving. Ariel pulled out her cellphone and dialed 911. "There's shooting at the dock. I think Pier 89." She paused.

"Oh, no. They're killing each other." Then she calmly closed the phone.

By the time police arrived with sirens blaring, several young men from both gangs were dead, including Kiyoshi.

"We can go now," Cindy said. The three of them crawled along the roof until it was safe to exit the building. They moved in the dark to the Escalade and drove to a seedy area not far from the warehouse.

"Why are we stopping here?" Cindy asked.

Without answering, Ariel took out a pack of cigarettes, lit one, stuck it back into the pack with the butt in and placed it on the front seat. "Come on, let's go home."

"What are you doing?"

"We needed a car and someone wants this one gone. Insurance, I think."

"Oh my, Ariel. What did you do?"

"You can get any service if you know where to look on the internet, I am just doing a service and using the car in the process." Behind them the Escalade had already started to burn. "Hurry."

"You took money for an insurance scam?"

"No, I told the person to put an envelope in the donation box of St. John's Catholic Church." Ariel laughed. "Just think how they will feel when they see a thousand dollars in cash in the box."

The next morning, Cindy used a rental truck to deliver clothing, shoes and household supplies to a local homeless shelter. Cindy hid her identity by wearing large sunglasses and baggy sweats. She kept the hood up on her hoodie. That done, she returned to the warehouse to help Nestor and Ariel finish loading the RV. With cash and documents hidden in various locations throughout the RV, Ariel turned to Cindy.

"I think it is time for us to go. I checked the news and it won't be long until they start heading to arrest Tiny. Then it's just a matter of time until they connect all of this to Takeo and the Oyabun." Ariel faced Nestor. "It's time to locate Takeo."

Nestor pulled up Mapquest on the computer. He input an address and printed out the directions. He handed the map to Ariel.

"Okay, let's go."

Cindy pulled out her phone. "I'll get an Uber."

"Whoa, sis. We have a car."

"Where?" Cindy's eyes opened wider.

Ariel squinted. "We have a car in the RV. Come, I'll show you."

The two girls stood by the RV and Ariel pushed a button. The side of the RV opened and revealed a sporty Miata.

Cindy smiled. "Are we taking that?"

"Oh, no. Too nice to take out on the streets. Our ride today is outside."

"You didn't agree to torch another car, did you?" Cindy groaned.

"No. I bought an old junker for today and then we just dump it when finished. It will probably be towed and crushed before we even leave town."

CHAPTER TWENTY-NINE

Nestor stepped in front of the sisters as they entered Tiny's bar. They rushed past the bar toward the back. Tiny came around the bar and blocked their path. "Where do you think you're going?"

Nestor faced him.

Tiny doubled over, his hands clutched his groin. He screamed and fell to the floor. Nestor stepped over the groaning man and pushed the door open in the back.

Both girls gasped as they gazed into the face of the man who took their parent's life. He held a gun and pointed it at the trio. His mouth opened but before he could utter a word, he dropped the gun and shrieked. He grimaced and grabbed his hand. "What the?"

"Sit down." Cindy commanded. Cindy, Ariel and Nestor moved further into the room and Cindy grabbed the gun.

Off to the right and behind a ornate oak desk, a large leather office chair turned slowly in the dark. Cindy pivoted, gun in hand and pointed at the chair. The chair stopped and revealed an elderly woman dressed in a red, satin kimono. The Oyabun.

Ariel and Cindy both gasped.

"You!" Cindy let the gun drop to her side. The old woman pulled a gun from under the desk and pointed it at the girls.

Ariel took a step forward and was shocked to see her own aunt sitting in the chair. "You, Auntie? You killed your own brother?"

"Step back." Oyabun commanded. She moved the gun to point at Ariel. "My brother? What a joke. He wanted to run the entire organization like a nursery. He wanted to get out of drugs and trafficking and turn legit." She pointed the gun toward Nestor. "Who's this idiot? And how did he disable him?" She motioned toward her man still cradling his hand and groaning.

"Why did you kill our mother? She had nothing to do with this." Cindy watched and waited.

"Your mother made your father get into the legitimate business. Stupid slut. I only wish I had gotten rid of you two earlier. Where have you two been hiding?" She got up from behind the desk, still pointing the gun. "Doesn't matter. Drop that gun."

Cindy dropped the gun with a thud.

Auntie moved forward and picked up the gun. She turned and fired several shots into Takeo as he lay on the floor. She stopped when the gun was empty. With her kimono she wiped the grip and handed it back to Cindy. "Now I have a case for self-defense. First, I'll take care of your dummy."

Nestor studied Auntie's bloodshot eyes.

"What?" She took a step back and made an unearthly sound, fear growing in her eyes. Then pivoted the gun toward her own face and fired. Cindy jumped back as blood sprayed on her and Auntie fell backward with a crash. Both girls glared at her dead body.

Nestor moved forward and took the gun from Cindy. He wiped it on the clean parts of Auntie's kimono and lay it next to the dead body.

Ariel glanced at her watch. "Come on. The police will be here soon. Time for us to leave."

CHAPTER THIRTY

Back at the warehouse, the trio packed up the last of their belongings. Both girls were quiet. When the last of the items was stored in the RV, they took one final look around. Nestor picked up Niko and headed to the garage. Ariel picked up a remote and she and Cindy boarded the RV. Ariel backed out of the garage and closed the door.

"Goodbye." Cindy whispered.

"Yes, goodbye to this chapter of our life." Ariel peeked into the back and saw Nestor was already shut down on a cot. The cat slept peacefully on his chest. "I don't know if I can even go through with the next part."

"I know," Cindy offered. "But then we are done."

Ariel slowed the RV when they were about two blocks away. She swiveled in the captain's chair and glanced at her sister. "Ready?"

Cindy nodded. She looked at Nestor lying on a cot. The cat purred softly. Then she noticed Nestor's hand moving slightly. He massaged the soft fur of the Persian cat. She nodded to her sister. "Let's step outside."

The girls got out of the RV and walked into the deserted street. Ariel took out the remote and pushed a button. The girls watched as the warehouse erupted in fire. "Won't be long now." Ariel said and got back into the RV. Cindy followed.

As they crossed the Hudson River, a large ball of fire could be seen behind them as the propane tanks exploded.

In the RV, Cindy leaned back in her seat. "I can't believe Auntie killed our parents and has wanted us dead all these years."

Ariel nodded but said nothing. She kept her eyes on the road. After ten minutes, Ariel glanced at Cindy. Cindy's eyes were half closed. "I guess we head for Huntsville now."

Cindy opened her eyes. "Yes, but let's take it slow, no need to hurry." She investigated the night, closed her eyes, and said nothing else.

Cindy opened her eyes to the bright sun. She sat up and yawned, "Where are we?"

"We're in West Virginia. I cut off Highway 81 and we're taking the 64. Then we'll catch Highway 40 in Nashville and take that into Texas."

Cindy paused. "Isn't that off the main route?"

"Yes, just a precaution in case someone tries to follow."

Cindy waited. "Why didn't you wake me? You want me to drive now?"

Ariel arched her back. "We'll stop in Morgantown and gas up and get some food. Then you can drive."

Less than fifteen minutes later, Ariel pulled into a Pilot Truckstop. Once fueled, they parked to the side and prepared to go into the restaurant. Before leaving the RV, the girls checked on Nestor. They found him sitting at the table. He was working on the laptop and did not look up.

"Leave him for now," Cindy said. "I need the bathroom and I'm starving."

Ariel shrugged and followed Cindy to the restaurant bathroom. The girls washed up as best they could and filled up on pancakes and bacon. Sated, they returned to the RV. Cindy went into the bathroom and changed into more comfortable clothes and hopped into the captain's chair for the journey. Ariel remained standing and watched her sister.

"What's wrong?" Cindy asked.

"Shouldn't we see what Nestor is doing?"

Nestor was still sitting with the laptop open in front of him. The sisters walked back to the table where Nestor sat. They slid in on both sides of him. Both girls leaned in to view the laptop screen.

"What is that?" Cindy asked.

Ariel clicked a couple of keys and zoomed out on the photo on the screen. She studied it carefully. "Oh. It's the Huntsville Prison layout in Texas." She leaned forward to look at her sister. "How did he know?"

Nestor turned his head, first toward Ariel, and then to Cindy. He reached up and gently tapped Cindy on the head.

"He read my mind." Cindy touched Nestor's hand. "You understand why we have to do this?"

Nestor nodded and returned his attention to the computer. Ariel yawned.

"Ariel, you're tired. You drove all night. Why don't we get moving and talk about this when we reach the RV park?"

"Hey, is Nestor's hair lighter?" Ariel raised her hands and stretched before she yawned again.

"Come on, Sis. You need some sleep." Cindy stood, went around the table and took her sister's arm. She helped her get up and walked her to the front of the RV. "Why don't you stretch out on the cot?" Niko soundly slept on the cot.

"No, let him sleep. I'll just sit in the passenger captain's chair." She got into the chair and leaned back.

Cindy checked the online map and started the engine. Ariel already snored softly. Cindy drove out of the truck stop and headed toward their next destination.

CHAPTER THIRTY-ONE

Cindy drove more than seven hours, only stopping once to fill the gas tank and use the restroom. Ariel remained sleeping the entire time. It was dark when she pulled into the RV park and checked in. She found her spot and connected the RV before going to check on Ariel.

Ariel opened her eyes and focused on her sister. "Where are we?"

"Elizabethtown, Kentucky at the RV park. You hungry?"

"Starving." Ariel swiveled in the chair and eyeballed the cot. It was empty. "Where's Nestor."

"Still at the back. Should we check on him?" Cindy got up and waited for her sister.

Nestor sat at the back table with his head down. Niko lay on the table next to the laptop. A half-eaten plate of cat food sat in front of the computer. Nestor's eyes narrowed and both girls jumped back. His hair was now a light brown. His eyes no longer had the upper fold of the Japanese but were Anglo in appearance and were a bright blue. A thin mustache lined his upper lip and his complexion was now sun-burnt.

Ariel went to Nestor and studied him. "Cindy, did you do this? Who is he supposed to look like?"

"I didn't do a thing. I'm not sure what's going on." Cindy also studied Nestor's face. "How did he change his looks?"

Nestor looked up and pointed at the laptop. The girls leaned in. A photo ID of a man who could be the current Nestor's brother stared back. Information on the ID card indicated the man was a guard at the notorious Huntsville Federal Prison. Ariel's stomach grumbled. Cindy lifted her head.

"Ariel, why don't you make us some sandwiches. I picked up some supplies when I last stopped for gas. I'll see what he is doing."

While Ariel busied herself in the kitchen, Cindy worked with Nestor. In a short time, Ariel returned with sandwiches of thick slices of ham, Swiss cheese on sour dough bread. She set the plates on the table with a bag of chips and two sodas. Niko immediately got up and began to paw at the sandwiches.

While Ariel fed small bites of ham to Niko, Cindy explained what she had learned so far.

Ariel peeked at the laptop and saw that Nestor had been texting a message to Cindy.

"Nestor knows all about our last assignment. He knows this is for Beth." Cindy said. "Even he can't explain how he was able to change but he's not done yet."

"Wow."

"The guard he chose is Robert O'Donnell. He works on the cellblock where the serial killer is housed. All we have to do is put the guard out of commission for a day and Nestor will be able to go in."

"That's it. Sounds easy. Not." Ariel frowned.

"Don't worry. Nestor is working out the details." Cindy dropped her head for a moment then peered at her sister. "I just want to put it out of my mind for a few hours." She picked up her sandwich and began to eat.

"Okay. We'll let him work on it himself. Still don't know how he was able to change himself." Ariel crunched on a potato chip.

"I wonder how Beth is doing?" Cindy popped open a soda.

CHAPTER THIRTY-TWO

Tom moved behind Beth, lifted her long red hair and kissed the back of her neck. She shivered. He moved around, leaned in and kissed her on the lips then sat next to her at the table. She remained quiet, leafing through a wedding magazine. A frown line creased her forehead.

"Having second thoughts?"

"Oh, no," she turned in her chair and put her arms around his neck. "I love you."

"Then what has you so sad?" His phone buzzed. He peeked at it and then put it back in his pocket.

Beth focused on Tom's face as if for the first time. "I was just thinking about Bill. I mean Dr. Thornton. I always thought he would walk me down the aisle." She leaned back in her chair. "I miss my brother, I miss James, I even miss Cindy. We were a family. The creation of Nestor has ruined us all."

Tom touched her hand, picked it up and kissed it. "I understand. I'm sorry."

"I miss my parents, too. If I had just let the hate in my heart go, maybe I could have helped them over the death of my sister."

"Honey. I'm so sorry." His phone buzzed again. He ignored it.

"Are you sure we are done searching for Nestor?"

Tom leaned back. "At this point, no one is looking for him and I think the government officials want to just put it behind them. There has been no word in months. No unusual deaths. No sightings. The Attorney General put a nix on the entire subject."

"But he could still be out there."

"Yes, that's true. But if he is not engaged in anything that gets the attention of the media, the government doesn't want to acknowledge he ever existed. Let's not let it ruin our day."

She forced a smile. "I'll be okay. Just feeling sorry for myself. I'm really very happy." She leaned forward and gave him a kiss. "Do you need to get your phone? Someone is obviously trying to get ahold of you."

He stood up. "Well, uh, yes. I'm so sorry. I'll just go into the living room and see who is calling." He left the room.

Beth heard the front door open and what sounded like muffled talking. "Tom?"

"Just letting the cat in. Be right there."

"Okay." Her eyebrows came together. "We don't have a cat." She got up and went into the foyer.

Her eyes widened and her knees trembled as she eyed Tom standing next to her brother and James. She ran to her brother and threw her arms around him. "Brad, what are you doing here? I thought you were in Iraq." She pointed to the duffle bag at his feet.

"It helps to have a future brother-in-law with connections." He smiled at Tom.

Beth turned to James. "And you, where is your luggage? Is Cindy with you?"

James took Beth into his arms and kissed her on the cheek. "My luggage is at my new apartment. Your fiancé had me brought back to D.C." He paused. "Much better job opportunities."

Beth jabbed Tom in the shoulder. "A cat, huh?"

Tom shrugged.

"Come on, guys. We have a wedding to get ready for."

James threw his arms into the air. "You have a fabulous wedding planner right here."

They all laughed.

"Hon," Tom turned to Beth. "There is still no trace of Cindy. Sorry."

"It's okay. I've got most of my family with me."

CHAPTER THIRTY-THREE

The next morning, Ariel and Cindy showered in the RV, ate a quick breakfast and prepared to return to the road. While the girls unhooked the utilities, Nestor stepped outside and glanced around. He had made a total transformation and now fully resembled the Huntsville Security Guard. Ariel came around the RV just in time to see Nestor heading across the highway.

"Cindy, come quick."

Cindy left the rear of the vehicle and ran to Ariel. Ariel pointed. "Nestor's heading to a church and it's Sunday. You have to stop him. What if there's another video?"

They watched as Nestor meandered between several cars in the church parking lot across the highway.

"Oh, no. You stay here. I'll see if I can stop him from getting into trouble." Cindy dashed across the highway, ignoring the bellow of a semi's horn.

Ariel held her breath and waited.

Cindy made it across the blacktop only to trip on broken asphalt along the road. Her jeans tore when she fell to her knees. The asphalt shredded her pants and scraped her knees. She ignored the pain and torn skin and jumped to her feet. The embankment was steep and she slid down then climbed over an old wood rail fence. Several splinters tore at her hands. Waist-high, yellowed weeds created a sea between her and the parking lot. Nestor entered the church. She sighed and plunged into the high weeds. Sharp edges slapped her as she waded through the spikes. Finally, she reached the parking lot and made her way through the cars. At the church door, she paused. The door squeaked as she pulled it open and entered the church. Voices raised in song as the congregation stood and sang Amazing Grace. Cindy finally spotted Nestor sitting in the back row on the right. She had forgotten he now had red hair and was much heavier.

Voices reverberated in the rafters as Cindy tiptoed to Nestor. She nudged him and when he raised his head, she mouthed "Let's go." He ignored her and moved over for her to come into the pew.

Cindy moved beside Nestor and again tugged at his shirt. He appeared to be mouthing the words to the song and ignored her. The song stopped.

"You may be seated." The Pastor's voice carried through the church.

Cindy nudged Nestor. "Come on."

Nestor turned toward Cindy and eyed the scratches on her hands and face. He studied her torn jeans, smeared with dried blood. He lightly touched her Levi-encased knee then peered into her eyes and took her left hand.

People in front of her seemed to float. Cindy closed her eyes. The room spun in her mind. She held Nestor's hand and floated above all the others.

Through her closed eyes, she watched a family sit down to a meager dinner of boiled potatoes. The father reached across the small table and they held hands. The father blessed their food and gave thanks for the love of their family.

The scene switched and a young couple stood in their living room. The young woman handed him a pregnancy test. He studied it for several seconds and then threw it in the air and hugged his wife. Together they danced around the living room, laughing. The scenes continued to cycle through Cindy's mind. She became dizzy and disoriented. Everything stopped and a young teen stood before his parents. He began to cry. He grasped a large dog collar against his chest. His parent moved closer to their son and held him in a tight embrace. On the fireplace mantel behind them a photograph of a graceful German Shepherd and the boy could be seen. The visions stopped and Cindy sank back into the pew. She opened her eyes.

The congregation stood and another hymn began. Nestor let go of Cindy's hand and nudged her out. She left the pew and together they hurried out the door of the church. Outside, they wove their way through the cars and were soon at the field of tall grass. Nestor scooped Cindy into his arms and carried her through the ochre reeds. At the wooden fence, he stepped onto a slat and easily climbed over, while still cradling Cindy in his arms. He stepped onto the asphalt of the highway, ignoring the protesting horns of the traffic. Once at their RV, he placed Cindy on her feet just as Ariel stepped off the stairs.

CHAPTER THIRTY-FOUR

Ariel placed her hands on her hips. She gazed at Nestor and her sister. "Well?"

Cindy ignored Ariel and followed Nestor into the RV. Ariel stomped her foot in frustration but went in after her sister.

Cindy stopped and nodded her head at Nestor, "I know what we have to do."

Nestor nodded, stood and went back to the laptop. He slid into the seat and began to type furiously. Cindy slipped in beside him.

She sighed loudly and Ariel sat opposite them. "Isn't anyone going to tell me what's going on?"

Cindy put her finger to her lips. She took the first page Nestor printed and started to read while he continued to type. "Can you get me a cellphone?"

"Will you tell me what is going on?"

"Get me the phone first." Cindy waited for the phone. "Ariel, why didn't we ever go to church?"

Ariel grabbed the phone and gave it to her sister. "What? What happened in that church?"

"Let me finish this and I'll tell you. I was just wondering why we never went to church."

"Maybe because our father was a Yakuza Oyuban." She paused. "I guess our parents should have introduced us to Buddhism, but it never happened. Why?"

"Let me make this call first." Cindy glanced at the printout and dialed. "Mrs. Knight? Hello, I'm Miss Wong from Granted Wishes."

Ariel mouthed 'Wong?'

Cindy shrugged. "I'm calling about the puppies you have for sale. We have a young man, Rusty Bowers, who just lost his German Shepherd, and we know you breed high quality Shepherds."

Nestor handed another page to Cindy. "Oh, you know Rusty and his family. That's wonderful. Yes, Lady Antebellum just passed away and his father had put in a wish for another dog." Cindy listened for several minutes. "Yes, Mrs. Knight, we know the family is struggling and we are willing to pay to replace his dog."

Cindy grabbed a pen and wrote several notes on the printed page. "Yes, we're not the far away and we can come by and see the puppy. Yes, I have information on our organization and you can make the paperwork out to the Bower family. Three thousand is no problem." Cindy wrote the amount on the page. "Really? You would like to come with us to present the dog. That would be wonderful. Okay, see you at two this afternoon. That will get us back to their home by the time Rusty comes home from school. Please don't mention this. Even Mr. Bower does not know his name has been chosen."

Cindy disconnected the phone and turned to Ariel. "Can you get out five thousand in cash? We need to pay for the puppy, buy some supplies, too. Then we'll give them a cashier's check for an additional thousand to care for the puppy."

"Then will you tell me what is going on?"

Cindy nodded and told Ariel about the vision of Rusty's loss of his dog and how she knew they had to make it right. "Ariel, you will need to change your appearance though. Don't think we want them to connect us as twins. Nestor will go in case we need to 'persuade' anyone."

Promptly at two the group arrived at Knights of the Roundtable kennels and met with Mrs. Knight. They showed the fake website printout Ariel was able to put together in under fifteen minutes and agreed to have Mrs. Knight drive her own car with the puppy in a carrier. When Mrs. Knight brought out the female shepherd and told them Lady Guinevere was actually a cousin of Lady Antebellum, Cindy knew Nestor had done his homework and no 'persuasion' was required.

At three-thirty that same day, Nestor, Cindy and Mrs. Knight stood on the porch of the Bower's home with Lady Guinevere in tow. Ariel waited in the car.

Mr. Bowers was somewhat hesitant about a granted wish, but Nestor was able to shake his hand and 'convince him' he had indeed filled out the application. Having Mrs. Knight there with the puppy with registration papers in Rusty's name appeared to make everyone happy. Mrs. Knight stayed behind after Cindy handed over a cashier's check for one thousand dollars to cover care and she and Nestor returned to the car.

Back in their compact car, Ariel waited until they were away from the farm before pulling off her wig and tossing it in the backseat with Nestor. She clapped. "That was so much fun. Why can't we just do this and forget about the final revenge?"

Cindy remained quiet.

Cindy parked the car next to the RV and let herself in. Ariel followed while Nestor extricated himself from the backseat.

Once inside, Cindy plopped herself into the driver's captain chair.

Ariel stepped in front of her sister. "So, why haven't you answered me? Why can't we just do good things and forget the mission?"

Cindy raised her head. "I would love to do things that would only help others. But I can't give up the mission."

"Why not? Don't you realize the plan may mean killing Nestor? What's wrong with you?"

Cindy gulped. "Nothing's wrong with me. We need to trust God."

"God? What are you talking about? You had one incident with Nestor and now you're a believer?"

"You don't understand, Ariel. It wasn't just one incident. I saw it all. It's not just about doing good. It's about understanding what is right and wrong. And we can't use Nestor to do it for us. We need to go out and do it ourselves."

Eyes wide, Ariel regarded her sister. "You're losing it, sis. You talk about doing something good, and yet you're willing to lose Nestor."

"I made a promise to Dr. Thornton. I can't turn my back on him. Besides, we can't keep Nestor forever. He's an android or did you forget?" Cindy swiveled in the chair and turned her back on Ariel.

"But don't you care about Nestor? He's not just an android, he's our friend."

Cindy swiveled back. He gulped to stop herself from sobbing. "I care about him, too. But you and I need to get on with our lives and we can't do that until this is over."

Nestor, stood behind Ariel and tapped his foot. Ariel turned in the passenger chair and Cindy lifted her head. Nestor looked at them and then went to the computer and began typing. They both heard the printer spit out a sheet of paper. He came back and handed it to Ariel. She read the sheet, dropped it to the floor and began to sob.

Cindy stood and retrieved the paper.

"No more fighting. Mission must continue. For Beth," the note said.

Cindy nodded at Nestor and then dropped to her knees and put her arms around Ariel. "It's okay," she cooed. "Maybe it is time to let him go."

Nestor picked up Niko, put the cat on his lap and reclined on the cot. He then turned himself off.

An hour later, they were back on the road headed toward Texas.

CHAPTER THIRTY-FIVE

Over the next two days, the sisters took turns driving. Little was said during this time. They stopped only to eat meals and refuel. When both were too tired to drive, they stopped at a truck stop and slept for a few hours.

Nestor took breaks to play with Niko and pet the cat's silky fur. Otherwise, he worked on the computer for hours. Since the girls were barely talking, they didn't bother to check on what he was doing.

About five on a Saturday afternoon, the trio checked into Trinity RV Resort not far from a beautiful lake and only twenty miles from the Huntsville Prison. They hooked up the vehicle, removed the Miata from the parking bay and parked it alongside the RV. Then the two girls shared a salad and fell into bed. Nestor stopped working, picked up Niko and went to his cot.

Early the next morning, Cindy woke to see Ariel dressed in a pair of slacks and a sweater. "What's up?"

"I found a church nearby. I want to take Nestor there."

"Ariel, why do you want to do that?" Cindy asked.

"Because you got to experience it. I think I deserve the same."

"But what if you see someone who needs help? You know we need to do this and leave."

Ariel bowed her head slightly. "Yes, I know. But I need to experience it too. Please let me go. I promise I won't get involved in anyone's life."

"Okay. You'll need to wear a disguise."

Ariel smiled and pulled a blond wig from underneath the counter. "I'm ready."

Nestor walked up and handed Cindy a stack of computer printouts. She leafed through them and nodded. Then she handed the papers to Ariel. "It's the plan, Ariel."

Without looking at the pages, Ariel put them down and turned to Nestor. "Yes, I know Nestor. The assignment or whatever you want to call it. It needs to be completed. But can we go to a church now?"

Nestor nodded at both girls.

Just after ten, Nestor and Ariel slipped into a church and slid into a back pew. They stood along with others and listened to a hymn being sung by the congregation. When the singing was done, Nestor sat down. Ariel sat beside him and reached for his hand. He took her hand and immediately her head dropped, and she took in the thoughts of others.

Visions of families engaged in everyday activities, children playing, spouses fighting and making up, swirled through her head. Then her sight settled on a couple. Though she could not see them, she knew they were sitting several rows ahead of her. Pain filled her mind and tugged at her heart. From the father's point of view, she watched as he threw open the garage door and found his daughter lying on the floor. The mother screamed and ran to her daughter's lifeless body. Ariel couldn't watch any longer and snatched her hand away from Nestor. She turned and hurried out of the church. Nestor followed.

When Ariel stepped into the RV, Cindy was sitting in the driver's chair facing the RV door.

"Well? How did it go?" Cindy asked.

Ariel dropped into the passenger seat and swiveled to face Cindy. "I think I understand now. I saw a lot of good things. Great families, children, relationships, etc. Then I saw a couple. I could not see their faces, but I could feel their pain. Their nine-year-old daughter was raped and murdered. It was awful." She took a gulp of air. "It was the mother's brother who did it."

Cindy reached over and touched Ariel's hand. "I'm sorry you had to see that, Sis."

Ariel surveyed her sister's eyes. "The pain they felt was incredible. I don't know how they survived." She paused. "They forgave him."

"Oh," Cindy sat back.

"It made me realize. As much as I want to, we can't play God. Even if it means losing Nestor." She looked over and saw Nestor on his cot, Niko purring softly on his chest. He stroked the cat gently.

Cindy nodded. "Time to finish it." She handed Ariel the stack of pages she had been reading. "You should read Nestor's plan."

CHAPTER THIRTY-SIX

Ariel pulled on the blond wig and posed for Cindy. "How do I look?"

Cindy laughed and handed her a pair of large sunglasses. "You look great." She adjusted Ariels' wig and stepped back. "Don't forget. Ask for a reservation at the back of the motel. I checked and they don't have any cameras. Any of the back rooms will be perfect. We can park the RV in an empty store lot half a block away."

An hour later, Ariel, followed by Nestor, walked into the Econo Lodge a few miles from the prison. Nestor stood back while Ariel went up to the counter and requested a room. "May I have a room at the rear of the motel? My husband has a bad sore throat and needs a couple of days to recuperate."

Nestor nodded and pointed to his throat.

The young girl behind the counter paid little attention as she had Ariel fill out a registration card. Ariel signed it as Mr. and Mrs. Robert O'Donnell and handed it back.

"May I pay for three days in advance?"

The girl nodded and took the cash. After giving Ariel her change and the key to a downstairs room at the rear of the motel complex, the twenty-something girl turned back to her Glamour magazine, totally ignoring Nestor and Ariel.

Once settled in the room, Ariel pulled out a burner phone and called Cindy. "All done. Room 7G. It's the very last room at the back of the motel. Downstairs, there's an entrance next to the back parking lot."

"I'll be there in an hour. But don't look for the RV. I rented a van."

"I thought we were keeping a low profile?"

"I used one of our fake IDs and credit cards and then paid in cash. Just look for a gray van. Should be there soon. I have the equipment inside."

Ariel and Nestor slipped out of the hotel room, crossed the parking lot and tapped on the door of the gray van. The van was parked at the back of the empty mall property under a large, overgrown and untended tree. Cindy opened the door, glanced around and ushered them inside. Two large laptops were set up and connected to a modem.

Ariel dropped into the seat across from one of the computers and scanned the system. "A portable satellite on the roof?"

"Yes, I disguised it to look like a luggage carrier."

Ariel turned toward her sister and smiled. "Got it. I just pulled up the prison system." She turned toward Nestor. "Can we get this all done tomorrow."

Nestor bobbed his head.

Just before six the next morning, Ariel parked their car on the side of the road leading to the prison. Cindy hopped out and Nestor unfurled himself from the cramped backseat.

After hiding Nestor behind some bushes a short distance away, she returned to Ariel. She pulled the wig down on Ariel's forehead and handed her a pair of dark glasses. "You ready?"

Ariel posed for Cindy. "Yes."

"You look like the girls he seems to like. Do you have the syringe?"

Ariel showed the syringe to Cindy.

"Be sure to keep the cap on until you need it. You don't want to accidentally inject yourself." As she walked toward the bushes, she called back over her shoulder. "I'll buzz you when I see him come around the corner." Cindy moved behind the bushes and was well hidden when O'Donnell's truck turned the corner and headed toward the Miata.

Ariel leaned into the open hood and pretended to inspect the engine. She turned toward the sound of the approaching motor and waved. The truck pulled behind the car and O'Donnell jumped out. At first, Ariel was startled by the appearance of the man who appeared just like the new Nestor. However, she collected herself, balanced herself on the high heels and put her hands on her hips.

"Need some help?" O'Donnell called as he removed his cowboy hat and approached Ariel.

Ariel smiled. "Yes, I think something is wrong."

O'Donnell moved around to the side of the car and started checking the motor. Once his head was under the hood, Ariel reached into her pocket and retrieved the syringe. She was ready to pull it out when Nestor appeared standing behind O'Donnell. O'Donnell moved from under the hood and turned.

"What the?" O'Donnell reached for the baton on his belt when Nestor put out his hand and touched him on the shoulder.

O'Donnell slumped forward and Nestor caught him as he crumpled toward the ground. Cindy ran out of the bushes.

"My God, Nestor." Then to Ariel. "Give me the syringe."

Nestor took the syringe from Ariel and put it in his pocket.

"Nestor, we need to sedate him and get out of here." Cindy said.

Nestor shook his head and removed O'Donnell's clothing. Within a few minutes, Nestor had on O'Donnell's uniform, belt and carried the prison access card. He waited.

Cindy nodded and gazed at Ariel. "We need to get him out of here and finish this. Give me the wig."

When Cindy was ready, together they placed O'Donnell in the passenger seat and put O'Donnell's cowboy hat on his head.

Ariel went to Nestor and hugged him. "I'll miss you, my friend." She turned and returned to the sportscar and stood by the driver's door. "I'll get the guard into the hotel room and tie him up." She turned to Nestor. "Are you positive we don't need to sedate him?"

Nestor just gazed ahead.

Ariel turned to Cindy. "Hurry back. I'll be waiting in the car."

CHAPTER THIRTY-SEVEN

Cindy picked up O'Donnell's keys from the ground and directed Nestor to hop into the truck. Together they headed toward the prison. She stopped the car before reaching the front gate and turned to Nestor. "Nestor, do you know what you are supposed to do?"

Nestor nodded.

"Okay. Be sure to give me some time to get back to the hotel, help Ariel with the guard and the van. So, let's say twenty minutes?"

He stayed still.

She reached over and touched his hand. "You know we'll miss you."

He took her latex gloved hand and nodded again. In her mind, she heard his voice and felt peace pass through her. *Miss you too.*

Cindy parked just past the gate and kept her head down as Nestor got out and went to the prison entrance. She didn't look back.

Nestor walked slowly toward the gate guard.

Cindy put the truck in gear and headed toward the hotel. She passed the site where they had taken Robert O'Donnell. There was no sign of the Miata, Ariel or the guard. She drove to the motel. The little red car was parked behind the motel out of sight between two semis. She jumped out of the truck and wiped everything down. She tapped on the motel door.

Ariel opened the door, a bottle of glass cleaner and a rag in her hands. "Great. You're here. I'm almost done."

Cindy glanced at the guard lying on the bed. Dressed only in a t-shirt and briefs, he snored softly. She placed the keys in a dish on a dresser. "How did you get him in here?"

Ariel finished wiping down the nightstand and turned to Cindy. "Not sure what Nestor did but it's like he's hypnotized. He does everything you ask and then just goes back to sleep. I actually got him to walk in here, take off his clothes and get in bed." Ariel pointed her gloved finger toward the chair. "I even had him fold his clothes."

"Great. We better get going. Nestor's already in the prison."

Ariel took one last look at the sleeping guard. "Do you think he is going to be okay?"

"Nestor wouldn't hurt him. We already know he is a good guy, so I'm sure Nestor wouldn't do anything that's permanent. Better grab those clothes. They're Nestor's." Ariel grabbed the pile while Cindy peeked at her phone. "We better get going. Nestor is waiting for us."

Nestor walked up to the gate and swiped his card. The duty guard smiled. "Hey, Robert. How goes it?"

Nestor pointed to his throat.

"Laryngitis, huh?"

Nestor nodded and the guard opened the gate and ushered Nestor in. Once inside, he made his way to a restroom near Block C where the death row inmates resided. He entered a stall and waited. While he stood patiently in the closed stall, another guard entered and used the urinal.

Sirens screamed throughout the prison. Nestor stepped out of the bathroom. Several guards, pulling on riot gear, ran past Nestor.

"Hey, you." One guard yelled as he hurried past Nestor's. "Something's happening. Everyone's being called to the other side of the prison. Get a move on."

Nestor tapped on the door in response and waited.

Cindy and Ariel sat in front of the computer in the van. Parked as far away as possible from the empty mall, Ariel logged into the Huntsville Prison security site. Cindy turned on another laptop and watched Ariel. When Ariel nodded, Cindy whispered into the microphone to Nestor.

"It's time."

Two security guards moved about the control center in panic. On the north side of the prison, cell doors were opening and closing. Prisoners, some tentatively, stepped from their cells to wander about the cellblocks. Neither of the guards noticed the only cells that opened were those of nonviolent prisoners.

Guard one, Gary Johnson, pushed numerous control buttons in an attempt to close the cells. Nothing. Guard two, Alan Spencer, tried the intercom system to no avail.

With the commotion at the other side of the prison, Nestor entered Block C. He moved from prisoner to prisoner. At Cell 9, he stopped and focused his camera on the occupant.

"That's Ramirez." Ariel leaned close to the screen. "What a slime."

Cindy picked up the external microphone and whispered. "Okay, Nestor we are ready for the download."

Ariel punched at several keys and sirens could be heard in the background. The girls watched as Nestor moved closer to Ramirez and the download could be seen on the bottom of Cindy's laptop. The red line moved rapidly and finally showed "Download Complete."

Cindy gave a thumb's up to Ariel and closed the laptop. She then began packing up items. Ariel logged off her computer and also began packing.

In the prison control room, Johnson and Spencer watched the security cameras. Chaos filled the prison as cell doors furthest away from Block C opened and closed at random. Several prisoners filed out as guards attempted to maintain control. The two guards watched in horror and called in for extra support.

"Hey, look at this." Johnson called to the Spencer. "O'Donnell is still in Block C. Looks like he's talking to prisoner Ramirez."

Spencer moved closer. He leaned over Johnson's shoulder and watched as O'Donnell appeared to take a shoebox-size package out of his shirt. "What the hell? How could he fit that in his shirt?"

Johnson panned the cellblock and jumped up as all ten cells opened at once. "O'Donnell's in danger."

Johnson grabbed the microphone. "We have to warn him." He yelled into the speaker for O'Donnell to watch out. His voice echoed back. "It's not working."

"Call someone else." Spencer screamed. "He'll get killed."

They stood helpless watching the camera as the prisoners moved closer to O'Donnell. With the most vicious criminals moving in on O'Donnell, the screen exploded in light and went dark. The security room rocked from the explosion and all the cameras went dead. Johnson and Spencer stood in shock.

As quickly as it started, everything was over. All the cell doors closed and remained that way. Guards had full control of the consoles and were able to get prisoners back to their cells.

With all prisoners locked up and accounted for, emergency personnel were brought in to sift through the damage on Block C. A small crater occupied the center of the circular cell block. Cell doors bent at angles and only a few cots were recognizable. Blackened bodies and parts littered the center of the room. Officials were on the scene with in thirty-minutes and medical personnel began removing the bodies while Alcohol, Tobacco and Firearms personnel swarmed the prison and started investigating the damage.

CHAPTER THIRTY-EIGHT

When the cameras went blank, Ariel reached over and hugged Cindy. Together they clung to each other and sobbed. Then Cindy inhaled, pulled back and looked at her sister through red-rimmed eyes. "Time to go."

Ariel wiped her face on her sweater sleeve and nodded. She isolated the download and attached it to a group email. When confirmation came through, she unplugged the laptop, removed the chip and slipped both into a Faraday bag. "Which car do you want to drive?"

"I'll take the van." Cindy pointed at the silver bag. "Did the emails go out?"

"Yes. The information should be hitting the desks of every FBI office in Texas and Washington, D.C."

"Good. I hope they don't take forever to get the information to Agent Ford. Then he'll make sure Beth knows." Cindy picked up a set of keys on the small table and handed them to Ariel. "You drive the compact. Meet you outside the car rental."

Both girls got up. Ariel opened the van door and peered out. The sun had set. "You sure you can drop off the keys?"

Cindy was already climbing into the driver's seat of the van. "Yes. We'll have to make sure we wipe everything down."

Ariel shut the door and walked to the small car. Her head hung low.

An hour later, the van was clean and the keys left in the overnight drop off box at the rental location. It would be weeks before the fake name and credit card were discovered. By then the twins would be far away from Texas.

Once the car was stored back in the RV, the girls headed West into the darkness.

Ariel sobbed as she drove.

Cindy reached over and touched her arm. "It'll be okay, Sis. Nestor won't be able to survive that severe of an explosion. We accomplished what Dr. Thornton wanted us to do. Now we are done."

Ariel nodded. "Yes, but I'll miss him. I had hoped we wouldn't have to destroy him."

"Me too."

EPILOGUE

The two attendants entered the morgue, each pushing a stretcher. One loaded a young male victim into a refrigerated vault and pushed the empty bed to the opposite side of the room.

"Boy, what luck. Only ten killed."

"Yep. Heard this guard took the brunt of the blast." The heavy-set man pushed Nestor's body into a corner. "God, he stinks. Smells like burnt rubber."

"Ain't you gonna put him in a fridge?"

"Nah. Those are reserved for people gonna be cut open. You think they gonna do anything with this pile." He zipped open the body bag and revealed the charred remains.

The first man made the sign of the cross and kissed the crucifix he wore around his neck. "I heard the guard was a good person."

"Lot of good it's gonna do him now." The second man turned away from Nestor and together the two men turned off the light and left.

In the quiet of the deserted morgue, Nestor's body shuddered as his skin healed. A brown crusted hand reached out of the bag and pulled the zipper the rest of the way down. Almost completely back to normal, except for darker skin, hair and eyes, Nestor stepped down from the gurney. He removed the tattered remains of his clothing and threw them into a trash container. Then he searched the room. In a refrigerated vault, he found the deceased body of a young man, killed in a terrorist attack in a mall. He removed the young man's clothing and stepped into them. From the back pocket, he took out the wallet and studied the driver's license. Twenty-two-year-old Brian Miller never knew what hit him. He was killed immediately.

Nestor glanced from the photo on the ID to the young man's face, now destroyed by the blast.

Good.

Nestor put his fingers on the young man's face. His own face changed and soon mimicked the young man on the table. Now he appeared like the photo on the driver's license.

Good.

Nestor returned to the gurney, pushed it across the room where others seemed to be waiting patiently for more victims. He then folded the body bag and placed it in a storage closet. That done, Nestor took a hooded sweatshirt from a nearby rack and put it on. He pulled up the hood and left the morgue. None of the personnel noticed the young man leave.

In Room 7G of the Econo Lodge, Prison Guard Robert O'Donnell woke up to find himself lying in a strange bed clad only in his shorts. He sat up and looked around, confused. His uniform was folded neatly on a nearby chair. He looked at his watch, checking the date and time. Two days had gone by. While he put on his uniform, he dialed his phone, which he had found on the dresser with his keys.

"Hey, boss. It's Robert. I must have tied one on. But I'm on my way to work now."

Robert found his bosses reaction stranger than usual, but grabbed his keys and headed to the prison.

In the Houston office of the FBI, the Director's secretary opened an attachment in an email to the Director. She watched the video for several minutes and then paused it and called the Director's direct line.

Three days after the explosion at the Huntsville Prison, Tom Ford was called into his supervisor's office in Washington, D.C.

Later that afternoon, Dr. Bethany Middleton-Ford sat at her desk designing a new prosthetic arm when Tom walked into her office.

"What are you doing here?" She asked.

He pulled a chair over and sat down next to her. "They found your sister's body."

Martha and Homer Brown travelled along the highway west of Fort Worth. Homer drove twenty miles per hour below the speed limit. Martha watched the barren landscape as they passed. Ahead she saw a man walking through the sand on the side of the road. A hot wind blew causing his light shirt to billow. She turned to Homer. "Look at that poor young man. In the middle of nowhere walking alone."

"Yup." Homer glanced over as they got closer.

"Shouldn't we stop?"

"You crazy? He could be a criminal or worse."

"So? Look at him. He doesn't even have water and its miles until the next stop. He could die out here."

"Ma, we're not supposed to pick up hitchhikers. Too many prisons around."

"But he could die out here." She insisted. They were almost adjacent to the young man. "And what are you worried about? Molly wouldn't't let anyone near us if they were dangerous."

At the mention of her name, the ninety-pound Doberman leaned over the front seat and licked Homer's face with a cold, wet tongue. He sighed. "Okay, at least we can give him some water."

He pulled the car over next to the stranger.

Martha pulled a bottle of cold water from a cooler at her feet. "Hey, young man, would you like some water?"

The young man turned and looked at the couple in the old car. His skin was covered in dirt and grime. What appeared to be a layer of ash covered his neck and hands. Molly moved to the window besides Martha and stuck her head out. The young man's hazel eyes moved to her and he took a step forward.

"She won't bite unless you threaten us." Martha explained. "You want some water?"

The young man put out his hand and let the dog sniff it. Homer noticed her stubby tail start to move back and forth.

"Where you headed?" Homer asked, leaning down to get a better look. The young man pointed West. "Don't talk, huh?"

The young man shook his head and pointed at his throat.

"Mute?"

The man, displaying a choppy haircut, began to pet Molly. The dog whined with excitement.

Homer laughed. "I guess you found a friend." He patted Molly on the rump. "Would you like a ride, son?"

By the time Martha and Homer pulled into a gas station in the next town, the man in the back seat had his eyes closed and Molly slept peacefully across his lap.

Printed in the USA
CPSIA information can be obtained
at www.ICGtesting.com
LVHW021415271223
767436LV00082B/2836